Frankincense, Gold, and Myrrh

Frankincense, Gold, and Myrrh

A Christmas Chrestomathy

Joseph Bottum

St. Augustine's Press
South Bend, Indiana

Manufactured in the United States of America.

1 2 3 4 5 6 29 28 27 26 25 24

Library of Congress Control Number: 2024940216

Paperback ISBN: 978-1-58731-244-1
ebook ISBN: 978-1-58731-245-8

∞ The paper used in this publication meets the minimum requirements of the American National Standard for Information Sciences – Permanence of Paper for Printed Materials, ANSI Z39.48-1984.

St. Augustine's Press
www.staugustine.net

For my daughter Faith
quaerens intellectum

Table of Contents

Introduction

I write about Christmas so much because that's where I perceive the thin place to be—the moment in which I sense most clearly the spiritual crossing over into the physical. The supernatural sneaking into the natural. The timeless visiting the timebound. The saints, I imagine, observe that phenomenon everywhere and feel it all the time. But the rest of us have to take the numinous where we find it.

This Christmas sense of richness—a thickening of reality in a thin world—is culturally bound, of course: set in a particular historical era, located in particular places and particular occasions. Other people may have different moments in which they feel the thickness of reality, other rooms in which to worship. But the individuality of Christmas memories, the specificity of the settings of Christmas stories and Christmas reflection, is not an indictment. We are human beings, forced by our physical existence to cobble our thoughts about the universal from our experience of the particular.

Maybe more to the point, the arrival of the divine in the mundane is the central and most outrageous claim of Christianity—that God entered the world, born a child in a cattle shed. This is what lends significance to history and importance to particular existence, and I have spent my life seeking (and usually failing to find) that significance and importance. It is, I suppose, a mysticism—but not the grand rising up into a merging into the divine, the loss of self in an ecstatic transport, the flight of the alone to the Alone. It is rather, at best, a mysticism of small things: an attempt to sense the reality of creation in the particular things that happen to come to hand.

And since Christmas is a place where I most often have that sense, down through the years I've written dozens of Christmas essays for magazines and newspapers: the *Wall Street Journal*, the *Weekly Standard*, *National Review*, and far too many more—to say nothing of the Christmas carols I've included in my poetry books. Along the way, Amazon asked me for contributions to their Kindle Singles series, and I wrote two short pieces of fiction about Christmas: "Wise Guy" and "Nativity." I intended to finish up the next year with a third installment, finishing up the stories' loose recasting of the legends surrounding the three Wise Men. Life intervened, however, and I didn't find the time or energy to start on that final story. Until now, that is. Life intervened again, but this time in the opposite direction, leaving me footloose and uncertain of what I should be working on. And in the empty space, I sat down and wrote the third story, "Port de Grâce," published here for the first time.

"Christmas is the illuminated path across the wilderness of life, our map to this world, and if we follow it—if we surrender, joyfully, to it— Christmas will lead us to where we need to go," I wrote in my 2012 memoir, *The Christmas Plains*. Returning to the nonfiction I've written over the years, the dozens of columns and essays I wrote for newspapers and magazines, I've selected, here in this new collection, a dozen—my twelve thoughts of Christmas.

Two themes emerged for me as I wrote about the topic over the years— two claims about how our attitudes during the Christmas season can become models for our attitudes "all the year 'round," as Dickens would say. I have, I know, a tendency to fall into sad funks and self-recriminations, and if I find the mad festival of Christmas an answer of joyous unselfconsciousness, well, who would be surprised to discover that all this appears in what I write about the season?

The first is the joy of the words. Christmas preserves for us an odd and fascinating vocabulary: Bethlehem and sleigh bells, crèches and chestnuts, Wise Men and mangers, Santa and tinsel, poinsettias and shepherds, candy canes and wreaths—all those words and phrases we know and yet employ almost only at Christmas. They have a glitter and an *oomph* to their meaning, from their association with the season. *Ha'penny*, for example. I use it only in the Christmas jingle about how Christmas is coming and the goose is getting fat. And because of that nursery song, the word *ha'penny* conveys to me still a strange little extra sense of the season, and charity, and God's love of the poor.

And why not? Why not have richer, deeper, more illuminated words? This is what we understood words to do when we were young and first learning language. This is the promise of what the medieval philosophers called the Unity of Truth: words and thoughts and reality all cohering, all growing together.

Maybe it's really true only in the words the angels speak as they sing hymns of praise around the throne of God, but we can surely do better with words than we have done. Poetry is what all language wants to be when it grows up—and our Christmas words have a kind of poetry built into them. Let that seasonal language, say I, be the model for how we speak and understand words all the long year 'round.

The second theme I stumbled on was the idea of spiritual geography. I do see the imperfections of the Christmas season in the way we celebrate now. Perhaps that's because I live in the wildly imperfect land of South Dakota, and the spruce and pines of the Black Hills just aren't the model cones and ideal shapes of the trees we used to shop for in the Christmas-tree lots of Washington and New York, the big cities I knew back east. Or maybe it's just because I'm imperfect and need an image of that even in my Christmas trees.

Like our Christmas memories, our geographies are more universal the more particular they are. The writings of the Church Fathers—the books of the Bible itself, for that matter—are filled with geographical metaphors for spiritual concepts. Should the Ark of the Covenant stay in the country camp at Shiloh or be moved to the city temple in Jerusalem? Is God best found in the lonely cell of a hermit out in the desert, or among the throngs of people in a crowded cathedral?

We can call these metaphors and symbols, for they are. But they are also something more than that. These are spiritual realities tied to the land and the home and the places where we have our being. Christmas, in our childhood memories, often has this more-than-symbolic feeling to it. My parents got a balsam tree for Christmas the year that I was five, or six, or seven. The memory is loose in time. But I remember with precision the strong scent and short needles and the stickiness of the sap. That tree is *located* for me, in the house out on the South Dakota plains, and it speaks to me still of a particular place and what it meant. And that, surely, is a universal experience. We live, through God's providence, in particular rooms on particular streets in particular towns that can have, that should have, a spiritual meaning.

I suppose, in the end, I write my Christmas stories, my Christmas essays, and my Christmas songs because I feel the disenchantment that marks our time. I need what we seem to lack here in late modernity—a living connection with the past, a density of reference, a thickness of vocabulary, and an external world that glows with cosmic meaning. And all that comes, at least a little, with Christmas.

Sources: The linked short stories "Wise Guy" and "Nativity" were published by Amazon in the Kindle Singles series. The third story in the "Gifts of the Magi" series, "Port de Grâce," has not previously appeared. The original versions of "Dakota Christmas," "The Poetry of Christmas," and part of "The Second Day of Christmas" appeared in the *Wall Street Journal*. "Oh, Tinsel," "Beyond the Bleak Midwinter," and "The Ghost of Christmas Past" in the *Weekly Standard*. "Christmas and the Boy Reader" and part of "The Second Day of Christmas" in the *Free Beacon*. "Angels I Have Heard on High" and "The Mind of the Magi" in *Law & Liberty*. "Joyous Surrender" in *Public Discourse*. "The Cold City" and "The End of Advent" in *First Things*. Intermediate versions of "Dakota Christmas," "Oh, Tinsel," "The End of Advent," and "The Ghost of Christmas Past" appeared in *The Christmas Plains* (Image, 2012). Portions of the introduction are drawn from Christmas interviews in *National Review* and *Patheos*.

Part One
Gifts of the Magi: Three Christmas Tales

Wise Guy

I

It all starts . . . but then, where does anything start? Back at the first moments of Creation, maybe, or down in some long-ago legend, its meanings and purposes faded now into the darkened past. Every story's opening is a little arbitrary, one way or another. Every beginning is a small lie.

Still, since this particular story concerns a thief named Bart Sagan, we should probably begin where he did—the afternoon of December 18, a week before Christmas, when he fought his way through the icy winds that slice down High Street to meet a friend at the Evergreen Tavern and ask her for some help. Hatch a quick plan with her, in other words. Plot a little crime.

So, as Bart laid out the story for his friend, it all starts when a drug runner for the local crime lord Harry King gets himself rattled—rattled good and hard, convinced he's only half a jump ahead of the cops.

Billy is that runner's name: Billy Euston. And maybe he's right to think the police are closing in on him. Or maybe he's just gone crazy. Who knows? Eventually, all drug runners start to hear footsteps, creeping along behind them, and they twitch in their sleep. But either way, there this scrawny, long-haired Billy character finds himself: abandoning his car on a south-side street to duck down an alley, lugging an old brown-leather suitcase.

Of course, with twelve three-kilo packages of heroin inside, the suitcase weighs almost eighty pounds. Both hands on the handle just to pull it along, wheezing like an asthmatic sheep, even Billy, loopy as he is, realizes he's not getting far. But up ahead, midway down the block, he sees a big delivery truck inching out of a gate. And it's then that Billy has the first of

7

his bright ideas: He'll throw off the police by slipping around the truck and hiding in the shipping yard.

Only trouble is, the yard's full of people: paper-baggers finishing their lunches, and smokers taking a nicotine break, and drivers standing around in little knots, shouting over the rumble of the trucks while they drink their coffee and wait for their loads. The place where he thought he could hole up for a while—dodge the police, maybe call Mr. King's people for a pickup—turns out to be the loading dock of a huge shipping center, a bustling madhouse in the middle of the Christmas rush.

It's not so much a plan as sheer momentum, as Bart explained it, that carries Billy forward into the building—red faced and sweating, jostled by the tide of workers: a scruffy kid in a leather jacket that's practically a sign on his back reading *Arrest Me, I'm a Criminal*, hauling a life-sentence load of heroin and trying to pretend he belongs there.

Inside, the shipping center proves even wilder. The last thing a paranoid, adrenaline-fueled drug runner needs is noise, and this place is *loud*. People yelling, forklifts banging around. An every-which-way tangle of conveyers— you know the kind of thing: those waist-high tracks covered with little wheels to help slide the packages along—all clattering away. The building is like a hundred-decibel pinball machine, and Billy's the ball, bouncing from bumper to bumper, tripping over people, stumbling into boxes, trying to find an exit. He notices a security guard down the aisle giving him the fish-eye, maybe, and talking into a radio, so he cuts back around an assembly line of workers packing up Christmas boxes for mailing and slips through a door.

Unfortunately, what he's walked into turns out to be a storage room, the shelves piled with empty white gift boxes, pretty gold bows on the lids. And it's there that Billy has his second of his bright ideas. He pulls down a dozen of the boxes, packs a bag of heroin in each, and stacks them on a rolling cart. Then he shucks his jacket and hides it behind the door with the suitcase. He puts on a stray blue apron, to match the workers he's seen, and grabs a dusty clipboard to look even more official.

A deep breath, and he's ready to go—except, trying to maneuver the cart out of the closet, he runs straight into a square-built woman, as immovable as a linebacker, wearing a red supervisor's apron. "There you are," she says, like she knows him, taking hold of the cart. "Where in the name of all that's holy have you been the last hour?" Billy tries to wrestle the cart away from her, but she's stronger than he is, there's a pair of security guards standing only five feet away, and she's shouting, "Susan, Bob, the rest of you, here are the last of them. C'mon, c'mon, people, the truck's waiting."

Susan and Bob—what looks like the whole assembly-line crew of packers—come running up, and before Billy can say a word, they've grabbed the gift boxes and packed them for shipping. The linebacker in the red apron snatches the clipboard out of his hand, glares at him, and marches off, yelling, "Here are the addresses. Let's go, people. Move, move, move." The security guards give him that sympathetic shrug men share when one of them has just been flattened by a woman, and there we are: Billy watches open-mouthed and helpless, gaping like a fish, while maybe $10 million of Harry King's property goes floating down the river of conveyor tracks, through a label scanner, and out the door as Christmas presents, scattered to God knows where.

He always wants to make it a story, Liz McCally grumbled to herself as her friend Bart paused his tale of some sad sack's misadventures to sip at the hot drink he'd ordered. That's his weakness. Bart's the best of us, maybe: smart, careful, always thinking ahead. Strong, too, with that kind of whipcord strength of a ranch hand who looks like he weighs a hundred pounds, dripping wet, but can master an unbroken horse in an afternoon.

Liz shivered a little, as she watched him across the table in one of the Evergreen's back booths, his long safecracker's fingers stirring his cider with a cinnamon stick. A thin, wiry man with a mop of black hair, handsome in an ugly, Abraham Lincoln way, Bart could be anything. Make a big score and retire, leave us all behind. But he wants it to mean something: to have a shape, reveal some purpose. He needs to turn everything into a story—a fable, capped off with a clean little moral—and eventually that's going to get him killed.

She liked Bart, she knew. Trusted him, would work with him on any parts of a job she understood. Maybe she was even in love with him, a little. But she wouldn't tell him that, wouldn't get tangled up with him, because it would hurt too much when the end they all knew was coming for him finally arrived, like a hearse pulling up to the door.

Swirling her own drink, studying his hands, Liz missed Bart's explanation of how Billy the Stupid Kid got out of the shipping center and reported back to Mr. King. Not that she cared about some drug runner she'd never met—or Harry King, as far as that went. She'd been a con artist in this town long enough to know the score: Anyone who crossed Harry King ended up knee-deep in the sludge at the bottom of the river, and Liz didn't figure she could learn water-breathing fast enough to escape with the kingpin's drugs or money, if she were fool enough to steal them. But apart from that, why should it matter? You didn't break into one of Mr. King's cribs, in the same way you didn't try armed robbery at a police station. Otherwise, you were free to take on any job you thought your luck and skill would carry you through.

"What's this got to do with me? With you, with any of us?" she demanded, while Bart stared off into the distance as though he were trying to see the end, see what it all meant—the Saga of Billy the Unlucky.

He looked back at Liz across the table, smiled that lopsided smile of his, and answered, "Yeah, well, that's the second part of the story."

Turns out, a couple of bruisers had picked up Bart that morning, scooping him off the sidewalk like well-dressed trash collectors just as he was leaving his apartment. Mute in the car, they stayed, as they drove him along. Not a word in the elevator and speechless down the marbled hallway, escorting him in silence through the mahogany doors and into the penthouse suite of Harry King—Harry King, in all his pomp and glory.

King looks, as Bart described him for Liz, like a pig farmer who's spent too much time around his animals. Greedy little eyes, quick and suspicious. The shrewdness of someone who knows how to get what he wants, and the impatience of someone who wants even more of it. The big, sausage-fingered hands of a man who likes to hold things and squeeze.

"You believe this?" King roars to the room full of people as Bart is shouldered inside, the doors closing behind him. A sycophantic little man in a black suit flinches as King swings a flashing necklace past him to wave above his desk. "A hundred-thousand dollars, that's what this little cockroach wants to charge me."

The drug world's unchallenged ruler narrows his eyes and stares for a moment at the flow of silver and diamonds like starlight around his hand. "Still, it's a pretty thing, and the wife will like it," he says, in a quieter voice. "All right, I'll buy it. Frank, take the cockroach outside and give him a check." He drops the necklace in a clump back into its velvet-covered case and hands it to the man on his other side. "Mike, put this with the other presents you're having wrapped. I'll give it to her at the party on the 24th, when all the bigwigs get their gifts. The rest of you, get the hell out of here. I want to talk to this man."

A thin, longhaired kid—cotton wads in his swollen nose and bruises forming on his face—starts to slide gratefully from his chair and join the exodus, till King jabs a fat finger at him and snarls, "Not you, Billy boy. Oh, no, not you. You stay and have a little conversation with us."

As the room empties, King comes around to the front of the desk and leans his buttocks back against it, waving Bart to a chair in front of him. "Sorry about that," he announces in the cordial tone that, in Bart's experience, usually means somebody is about to point a gun at his head. "Christmas Eve Day—is that how you say it? It sounds wrong, somehow." He gives Bart a puzzled look, then lets it go. "Anyway, the afternoon of the 24th, I'm throwing a reception for the mayor, the head of the museum, maybe the D.A., a dozen of the real powers in this town. 'Establishing respectable credentials,' my lawyers call it."

He shifts against the desk and stares over Bart's head at the books like wallpaper on the shelves at the back of the room. "Funny thing about respectable people," he adds. "You can give them money—you *have* to give them money: lots and lots of it, all quiet and discreet for their charities, if you want them to let you into their respectable world. But if you try to give them something sensible as a little goodwill gift, a watch or a car or something like that, they lean back all insulted and sniff like a maiden aunt who's just heard a dirty word."

He sneers, "What you can give them, though, is food. It's the *social* thing to do, the lawyers tell me: a little gift for the household to show your heart's in the right place. So that's what they're getting from Harry King for Christmas." He points over at the other side of the room, and Bart twists around to study the long table piled with tins and bottles and half-wrapped presents. "Caviar, truffles, Japanese mushrooms, crap like that. Coffee at $400 a pound from Sumatra or some damn place. A $1,000 bottle of wine. $5,000 a box, that's what these little house presents are costing me, and none of it worth the pot to piss it away in. But respectable, yeah—oh so *respectable*."

Then Harry King shakes his head like a horse chasing off a fly. "I'm talking too much. You're a busy man, so let's get down to business. This," he says, waving his hand toward the kid in the chair, "is Billy Euston, and he's lost something that belongs to me. He's my sister-in-law's nephew, and I'd never hear the end of it if he fell down a flight of stairs and broke his neck. So maybe Billy isn't going to pay as much as he should for yesterday's mistake—at least, not if you can fix it for him. Take him with you when you go, and he'll give you the details about how he mislaid my property."

Bart opens his mouth to ask why he needs any details at all, but King holds up a finger again. "Here's the point. I know all about you, Bart Sagan. I know you're maybe the slickest thief in my town. *My* town. I know you've got a little crew of friends and helpers that you'd hate to see anything happen to. Little Liz McCally, for instance, as pretty as a picture. Be a shame if she got hurt. The bartender down at the Evergreen who passes messages for you. All the rest of you independents."

He sneers again. "All the rest of you small-timers. I've let you work, let you go about your business, for too long. But now it's tax day, all over the city, and your bill just came due. Get my property back for me, and we'll call it even."

Groping behind himself for an envelope, he adds, "The police don't know anything yet, don't have a clue about what's happened, and I want it kept that way. That's why I'm using you, instead of my own men, for this job. You have a reputation for being quick and quiet, not making waves—so find my property, quick and quiet. What's today, December eighteenth? I want it all back before New Year's." Then he tosses the envelope into Bart's lap. "Here's some money, a few thousand, for expenses. And maybe there'll be a little bonus, if you get it done right, with nobody ever knowing. But that's all."

Harry King smiles, an emperor surveying the world he owns. "It's tax day, Bart," he repeats, rolling the phrase around in his mouth like he's tasting it for the first time and deciding he likes the flavor. "Tax day, and everybody everywhere is going to pay. Now take Billy here with you and clear out. I've got work to do."

So Bart rises from his chair and leaves the penthouse, trailed by the hangdog Billy, much as Harry King's bruisers had brought him: never having said a word.

II

By the time Cicely D'Angelo caught him in her house—by the time he'd danced with her to a scratchy old record on the phonograph, and kissed her white hair in the light of a Christmas tree at the record's end—Bart knew the job was going wrong.

Not that it hadn't begun well. The con that Liz ran at the shipping center, for example, proved easy enough. A brown delivery uniform was enough to get her through the door, she told Bart as she handed him the mailing list at noon the next day, December nineteenth. After that it was just a matter of a little strategic cleavage, a few tears welling up in her eyes, and a helpless-maiden tale of a dozen ruined addresses that she was going to get fired for, if she couldn't replace them. In by 9:00 that morning, out by 10:00, a printout of the list in her pocket.

"The guy who helped me, digging out the names and addresses from their computer system, is some kind of geek genius. Better even than you, Bart, and I always thought you were good. He'll end up running the place, if he can learn to keep his paws on his keyboard." Liz smiled indulgently. "He even discovered where the names came from—a page of entries in an advertising campaign from a couple of years ago. He was starting to wonder why they were popping up again, all in the same order, for a Christmas mailing this year, but I managed to distract him." She smiled again. "He's already left me a message, asking for a date."

Bart studied the list for a moment or two before setting it down on the tavern table. He sighed, staring at his drink as he stirred it with a thin pink-and-white swirled stick.

"What is it?" Liz asked.

"Hmm? Oh, this? It's schnapps with a peppermint candy cane," he answered. "I always order hot drinks in December. They taste like Christmas, somehow."

"No, you idiot," Liz snorted in exasperation. "Not the drink. The *list*. Did you see the kicker?"

Yes, Bart had seen it, like a boot to the head. Nine addresses in the city, two in the nearby suburbs. Or nearby enough, anyway, that maybe he could complete the whole assignment in the days he had left before people started opening their Christmas presents. Break into eleven places without leaving a mark, locate the boxes, replace the heroin with something the same weight so the victims never knew they'd been hit, and then slip out again unseen: unlikely, but at least imaginable. But the twelfth address—that was impossible.

"How am I supposed to get all the way out to Minnesota and back in time to steal the rest of the packages?" he asked Liz. "For that matter, where do you suppose it is—this Port de Grâce place?"

"Up near the Canadian border," she answered smugly. "Population 2,412. Major industries: timber and mining. Lots of ice fishing. The local high school—the Fighting Beavers—won the Minnesota Division II hockey tournament last winter and are favored again this year, if their goalie gets over his mono in time. Some of the girls on the chat networks think he caught it kissing that cheap, bottle-blonde cheerleader from International Falls, but they admit they don't know for sure. What are you staring at? I looked up the town online."

Bart laughed for the first time since Harry King had laid down his orders. "The trouble is," he explained, "I don't know any good thieves out in the middle of the country. Someone from here will have to go, and it's almost impossible to get people for a serious out-of-town job this time of year. After the holidays, they're all broke and hungry, but before Christmas—that's the one time they worry about being away from their families."

"I guess," said Liz slowly, "we could try this guy I grew up with in the foster home, if you want. His name is Johnny. Johnny Jasper. He called the other day, looking for work. He's steady, even if he is kind of a doob."

"A doob? Is that like a dweeb?"

"No . . ."

"A dork? A doofus?"

"C'mon, Bart. You know what a doob is. It's a . . . a *doob*. It means—oh, I don't know. It means he's unlucky, maybe. Like, if a job falls apart, you just know he'll be the one who gets caught. But he won't steal from his partners, and how tough can that place be? I mean, we're talking small-town

Minnesota, here. Not New York or Los Angeles. The only worry is that they'll mistake the stuff for powdered sugar and use it to bake a cake for him."

He liked Liz, Bart knew: liked her spunk, liked her quickness. Liked her looks, too, he had to admit. Small, five-two or -three, maybe, and over-flowing with all-American cuteness—a cuteness she relied on in far too many of her scams, especially that girl-in-distress routine she would run on anything even vaguely male. But her face: It hinted at something more. Something reaching toward an individual character, an individual beauty. Her bright eyes, her hair . . . He caught himself studying her and jerked his gaze back up toward the tavern's front windows.

Unfortunately, Bart also knew that working with Liz led to trouble. She'd gotten the lucky bounce so often, she'd come to believe that luck ruled the universe, and it lured her out ahead of herself—hurrying a job, throwing off the timing. Oh, she appreciated competence, even in some-body like the shipping company's computer guy. But in the end, she divided the world into the lucky and the unlucky, and she pushed too hard. She's like a tennis player, Bart reflected, with no strategy except to rush the net and take the ball on the volley. You can win a lot of points that way, steal a quick set of games, but you tend to lose the long, drawn-out matches, with-out ever quite understanding why.

Bah, he thought, this business is making me sour. On any given job, you trusted Liz for what she was good at, and you kept her out of the rest. And why not? She was looking for her path, like everyone else. We're all stumbling around in the dark, seeking even the faintest glimmer in the sky to follow.

"How much does a kilo weigh?" asked Liz, interrupting Bart's reverie.

"A kilo—what do you mean, how much does it weigh? It weighs a kilo. A kilogram."

"No, I mean how much does it weigh in some normal weight? You know, like a measure we normally use. How many pounds?"

"Oh. Just over two pounds. A kilo is 2.2 pounds."

"Okay," said Liz. "Now we're cooking." She turned to look over her shoulder at the Evergreen's bartender. "Hey, Tim," she called out. "How much does a liquor bottle weigh? Like a regular bottle of wine?"

"Full? Three, maybe four pounds," he answered. "Depends on how thick the glass of the bottle is."

"Thanks," she called back. "So how about that?" she turned again to ask Bart. "Three kilos in each box, 2.2 pounds a kilo, that's 6.6 pounds. Call it six and a half. Two bottles of wine the right weight, and we've got what we need for the swap. Nobody's going to be too surprised by getting wine for Christmas, right? No more surprised, anyway, than they are simply by the fact that someone sent them an anonymous present."

"Yeah, maybe," answered Bart. "Stop by the liquor store, and see what you can find. Meanwhile, I think I'll drive out to the suburbs this afternoon. I've got to start looking at these places, figure out which ones are going to be hard to break into. See if I can put together a plan."

"What else do you want me to do?"

"Nothing. Tell your Johnny friend to call me, and I'll fill him in, set him up with a plane ticket, get him moving. But otherwise, I want you out of it."

"I'm already in it," Liz snapped. "Harry King put me there when he threatened me and everybody else we know. You can't protect us. Not from King. Not from anybody."

"C'mon, Bart," she added, softening. "I know you want to be Santa Claus, bringing comfort and joy to all us little wide-eyed children, amazed at how wise and wonderful you are. But even Santa has his reindeer and those goofy elves helping him out. Let me call around, find out which of our friends are in town, see if I can't talk one or two of them into giving us a hand. At least we can be good little elves and scope out the addresses here in the city for you."

"No breaking in? No jumping ahead? Just checking on them?"

"Cross my heart," Liz swore, drawing an X on the front of her brown uniform blouse, the look of innocence on her guileless face a greater promise of dishonesty than anything Bart had seen in years.

Maybe Liz has it right, Bart was beginning to think. No hesitation, no planning. You just walk in and try to make something happen. At least, that's the way it worked at the second house he went to check. Wearing a dark green gas-company uniform pulled from his trunk, he'd driven slowly past the first of the suburban addresses—formulating, as best he could, an idea for how to hit the small, green bungalow.

The second address, however, turned out to be up a long drive extending from a quiet suburban street. The previous weeks of ice and snow, piled up by the plows in long hedgerows, masked the property boundaries, and before he fully realized he was on the estate, Bart had come around the curve of the drive, in full sight of the front door.

An old-money kind of house, it seemed, belonging as if by right in this old-money kind of suburb. Maybe it had been a little gaudy, back in the day, but the mainstream of American architecture had long ago flowed past it, and the place now looked almost stodgy—the pretensions of the exposed beams, fancy stucco, and leaded windows softened by the thick ivy slowly enveloping the house and the big trees that had used the years to grow up around it.

Standing on the wide steps, her arms wrapped around herself for warmth, was a woman in a gray dress and white sweater, arguing vehemently in Spanish with a man in a parka, holding a shovel. The housekeeper and the groundskeeper, Bart guessed, with different ideas about what needed to be done. Not even the arrival of a stranger halted their squabble, and as he stepped from the car to offer some spiel that might account for his presence, the woman merely glanced at his uniform and waved him around to the side of the big house where, presumably, the gas meters were to be found.

Much as Bart disliked being seen by his targets, the chance to check out the security system was too good to pass up—and the chance proved even better than he had supposed. A window at eye level, in what looked like a pantry. Visible through the window, a white Christmas box with a gold bow on top, sitting in a nest of brown-paper packing material on the counter next to piles of sorted mail. And a few feet to the right, a side door opening into a deserted kitchen. Unlocked, too, he discovered when he gave the handle an exploratory turn.

Now, think of that: an open door in what felt like an empty house. It's hard to say what more of a welcome sign a thief could want in this life. A few quick steps down the hall, the bag of heroin lifted out of its box, some jars of fancy foods off the pantry shelves put inside to give a rough match of the weight, and the lid set carefully back on. Out again through the side door, the tape-reinforced plastic bag hidden down against his hip. A ducked head and a wave at the still-arguing couple, and Bart had successfully completed the first of the tasks Harry King had demanded of him.

He smiled as he paused his car at the bottom of the drive to tuck the heroin under the passenger's seat and look again at the shipping list. The twelve crimes of Christmas—now eleven, he noted with satisfaction, crossing out the name and address of one Michael Stuyvesant: the victim of a smash and grab so lightning quick and honey smooth that, with any luck, he would never even know he'd been smashed and grabbed.

Hubris was the term Bart later used to describe it: the confidence he felt after the Stuyvesant job, the sense of invincibility that led him to drive straight back to the first of the suburban addresses—the little green bungalow with the drooping eaves that belonged, according to the shipping list, to a woman named Cicely D'Angelo—and try his luck at a second daylight felony.

Of course, since the person to whom he eventually told the story was the battered drug-runner Billy Euston, who wouldn't know the word *hubris* if it slapped him (as his distant relative Harry King had, several times), some of the point may have been lost. But picture it this way: On Bart's first pass down the street in the failing afternoon sun, the house looks quiet and deserted, with no car in the driveway and the white Christmas-tree bulbs through chintz curtains the only interior lights he can see. So he parks around the corner, straightens his gas-company uniform, and walks up to the house, as bold as brass.

There's an odd, threadbare quality Bart could sense, he tried to explain to Billy, even on the front porch. The fading paint, the suet hanging in a rusting wire basket for the cold birds, the aging wood of the window frames—they should have told him something, should have warned him. But the lock on the front door is a museum piece, almost an insult to a modern thief trained up on electronic alarms, and a few seconds with his picks is all he needs to tickle it open and slip inside.

Threadbare. It's one of those words that's almost a story, all by its lonesome. The wingback chairs, the patterned rugs on the wood floor, even the parson's table in the entryway, loaded with knickknacks and seemingly designed to trip an unwary thief—they're all a little worn or frayed: not dingy, exactly, or dusty; well cared for, in fact. But they suggest, somehow, that they've seen better days. That the world itself, maybe, has seen better days.

Peering carefully around the corner, Bart spies in the front room a Christmas tree straight out of an old magazine advertisement. You know the kind: pewter and glass ornaments dangling down. The fat bulbs of old-fashioned white lights, swirled like soft ice-cream cones, clipped on the branches. A bright star on top. And there, among the smattering of small presents on the red skirt around the base of the tree, waits a white box with a bright gold bow.

As he moves toward the tree, Bart finds himself inching past yet another crowded table, this one overflowing with a crèche: shepherds, Wise Men, the Holy Family—joined by a stampede of small wooden, stone, china, and even metal animals. It's as though the remnants of a dozen old Noah's Ark sets had decided, all at once, to go and gaze upon the Infant Jesus. Elephants, camels, giraffes, horses, raccoons, and porcupines. Wildebeests, wolverines, and wombats, for all that Bart could tell. The mass migration filled the table, while from the cliff top of a neighboring upright piano, a second wave of the menagerie looked down in wonder.

"They are rather a jumble, aren't they?" pipes a small voice from across the room, freezing Bart in place. "But each of them was a gift from a student, and how can I have Christmas without setting them out? I'm sorry. I must have nodded off here, waiting. Oh, Tommy, what took you so long?"

III

Ninety, she must be, Bart told Billy. Ninety, ninety-five, a hundred, who could say? Old, anyway, and white haired, a tiny figure curled up in an upholstered chair across the room, with a faded tartan throw rug draped over her.

"Forgive me," she adds. "I'm always a little at sixes and sevens when I wake up, these days. You're not Tommy, of course. Come help me up, dear, and we'll put on some tea."

And so, in a kind of daze, master thief Bart Sagan threads his way across the room and eases Cicely D'Angelo, as fragile as a winter bird, up from her chair and into the kitchen.

"There we are," she begins to prattle. "Now, let me put on the water, and if you wouldn't mind, the cups and saucers are in the hall, in that awful old cabinet of my mother's. It's silly of me, I know, to keep the monstrous thing, with the house already crowded. But my mother was so proud of it. Remember? She had it in the parlor, where every visitor could see it, there in the house on Stilton Avenue when I was a girl."

She turns and smiles at Bart. "No, how foolish of me. Of course you don't remember that house. You really must forgive me my rambling. A strong young man like you: You're too busy to know, naturally. But eventually, when life slows down, you'll find the past survives mostly in old things. Old things and the memories they hold. Cabinets, pieces of jewelry, those Christmas animals: Every one of them has a story it wants to tell. A story it *does* tell, most days. Chatter, chatter, chatter. I tell you, some days I think I will go mad, the house is so full of noise."

Bart nods and steps toward the front of the house. He intends, naturally—*naturally*, he paused his story to point out the word to Billy: a few moments trapped with the old lady, and he's already saying things like *naturally*—to slide straight out the front door. But then Cicely calls out, "Don't forget the creamer and the sugar bowl, dear. We'll use the porcelain my sister Amelia painted, with all those silly little flowers on them. Anemone, asphodels, and China asters, if you can believe it."

Which makes Bart stop to look through the upper glass doors of the cabinet at the sets of dishes, and before he quite understands why, he's picking out the pieces of the fragile tea set and ferrying them to the kitchen. "Leave the teapot here, dear, and arrange the rest on the small table in the front room, if you would be so kind. Napkins in the dining-room sideboard," Cicely adds kindly.

Of course, then he has to make an additional trip to the dining room for the silver. A journey to the kitchen for a platter of cookies and the hot teapot. Yet another trek to the hall for the plates he had forgotten on his first visit, and by the time everything is arranged and Cicely is perched on her needlepoint chair to pour the tea, Bart has begun to feel that maybe he really could use a snack.

"Star-of-Bethlehem, that's for atonement, isn't it?" asks Cicely, while Bart tries manfully to get an actual swallow from his delicate cup. "A pink rose stands for grace. Morning glories mean 'I love in vain.' Do you know the language of flowers, dear? Our mother taught it to us when we were young, but I can't quite remember what these painted flowers of Amelia's are supposed to be saying. Something sad and heartfelt, no doubt. Amelia took such joy in being melancholy. What a beauty she was, the boys swirling around her. But she always danced away, a tragic smile on her face as though they had broken her heart—instead of the other way around."

She gazes down at the tea table until at last she murmurs, "*There's rosemary, that's for remembrance. Pray you, love, remember. And there is pansies, that's for thoughts.* Shakespeare knew the language of flowers, of course. *There's a daisy. I would give you some violets, but they withered all when my father died.* Oh, Tommy, do you remember those purple lilacs you brought, the first time you came calling? So sickly sweet, a boy's fantasy of what flowers should be. I thought they were for Amelia, but no, my father said, a young man had brought them for me."

She closes her eyes for long enough that Bart thinks to make his escape, imagining she's fallen asleep. But his teacup rattles as he sets it down, and Cicely returns from her memories. "All done, dear?" she asks. "Help me clear these dishes away, then, and you can tell me why you've come."

The funny thing is, he's tempted to tell her the truth. Oh, while they're cleaning up—Cicely washing at the sink, Bart drying beside her—he tries out his story of being just a man from the gas company, stopping to read the meter. But Cicely merely answers, "Are you, dear? That seems unlikely," and sends him back to the dining room to put away the silver.

And by the time they're settled companionably in the front room, Bart has fallen into a kind of wondering resignation, fiddling with a small bowl of beads on a side table and waiting to see what comes to pass.

"I can't think how many years I've saved those. Glass beads, nothing fancy, of course, but, oh, I felt so fine wearing them. A young man named Tommy was coming to take me to a ball at the college, and my sister Amelia went out and bought me a necklace to wear. Tommy and I drove in a taxi—my first taxi ride with anyone except my father—and we danced and danced. Such dances, and he kissed me. But the necklace broke, and those loose beads in the bowl are all I could gather up. I still remember how they looked, glittering there on the polished wood floor of the ballroom. It was just an inexpensive little thing, but I sometimes think I've spent the rest of my life searching for the lost pieces."

She smiles and meets Bart's eyes across the table. "And you, dear? What are you searching for? I can tell, you know. There's something you're pondering, there in your heart."

So, almost in a dream, Bart tells her. Tells the white-haired, bright-eyed Cicely D'Angelo the whole thing: the story of Billy, the accident-prone drug runner, and the tale of Harry King, the brutal overlord, making a play for respectability even while he taxed the town's criminals. The untrustworthy cleverness of Liz McCally, drawn into the plot. Her worrisome foster brother, the doob Johnny Jasper, heading off to Minnesota to retrieve a distant package. Even the break-in he had committed that afternoon, lifting three kilos of heroin from beside a stack of medical bills in the pantry of Michael Stuyvesant's empty mansion—Bart explains it all.

"Why would you do that?" Billy interrupted to ask when Bart reached this point in his story. "I mean, that's crazy. I don't get it. I don't get it, at all."

"I know, Billy," he answered. "But that's why I'm telling you all this—because you haven't been getting it. And the time has come for you to start."

After Bart finishes describing the world closing in on him like a vise, Cicely nods and says, "It's a puzzle, isn't it? Put on some music, over there in the corner, while I straighten a little and see if I can't think of some advice for you." She struggles up and adds, "The difficulty is really your friends, isn't it? Holding them safe? Yes, we have to find some way for you to keep watch over your flock. And that awkward young man who lost the packages, as well. He's come into your life, the poor sheep, and now you must take care of him, too."

So while Cicely putters among the bric-a-brac in the front room, each of the animals in the crèche's long procession receiving a dusting, Bart examines the records on the shelves beside the ancient Victrola in the corner—a stand-alone phonograph player, built into a polished wooden cabinet. The Andrews Sisters and Vic Damone are there. Dinah Shore. Perry Como crooning "Some Enchanted Evening," and Nat King Cole emoting his way through "Nature Boy": *The greatest thing you'll ever learn, / Is just to love and be loved in return.* Peggy Lee, Bing Crosby, the Mills Brothers—a meandering through long-gone decades of popular music. Pulling out a Christmas album almost at random, Bart slides the record from its paper sleeve and sets it carefully on the turntable, the music rising just above the low hum of the tubes warming up in the old machine.

"That's lovely, dear," Cicely calls. "Now come help me dust while we put our heads together. My father was a lawyer, you know, and I remember some of the gangsters who would come to speak with him. So dashing, my sister and I thought them, in their stylish suits and hats. But not always the brightest of men. Shrewd in their own way, no doubt, with an eye on the main chance, but no, not terribly good thinkers."

Bart beside her, straightening the crèche, she adds, "And that's your problem, isn't it, dear? Oh, you're one of the sharp ones, I can see. But it's not enough to be smart. You also have to be wise." She pauses, and in the background, Bart could hear the soft singing of a carol, *Bearing gifts we traverse afar.* "Not everyone has that chance, you know. Up on the piano, toward the front, do you see a pair of elephants? Carved from some African tree, I believe. One of my students gave them to me—sent them from overseas for Christmas, long after I'd taught him in school. Such a lovely boy."

She studies the small wooden animals Bart has risen to take down for her. "Yes, a lovely boy. Gone now, of course," she sighs. "Every few years, while I was teaching, I would have one of you in my class, you know. Bright boys but distant, their eyes always focused off on the horizon as though they were searching for something to lead them. As though they were watching for a sign."

"Ah, well," Cicely adds, her voice tiring. "Set these back on the piano, dear, and let's finish here. They say elephants never forget, and perhaps that's my problem—not forgetting. I wish I could tell you what to do, but one feels one is not really allowed, these days. Except perhaps for this: Try to be wise. All you bright young boys, so intelligent and lovely—you need to learn to think not only *how* but also *why*. Yes, don't be afraid to puzzle it through, finding what it truly means. And along the way, see if you can't find a different star to follow. Your gifts were given you for better things than this." She leans against Bart and murmurs in exhaustion, "Oh, and marry the girl, dear. There will be time enough to be alone. Time enough, Lord knows."

As Bart guides her back across the crowded room to her chair, Cicely begins to sway in time with the last song on the record, a melody he can't quite remember from the distant edge of childhood. "Oh, Tommy," she whispers, "I knew you would come back to dance with me again. Why did you stay away so long?" And there in the final strains of the soft music, he kisses her hair and covers her gently with the blanket as she falls asleep again, as light as snow.

A step across the room to turn off the Victrola, a reluctant stop to kneel down, removing the bag of drugs from the box beneath the tree, and Bart pauses in the doorway to look back at her. "I wish I could have been Tommy for you," he says quietly. "I wish he had come back."

"I know, dear," Cicely D'Angelo surprises him with a last answering whisper. "But Tommy was lost in the war, ages ago. Ages and ages ago. Be well, my love. Be wise."

IV

Even at the early afternoon hour when the gray city sky was as light as December would allow it and most of the town had finished lunch, each as each could, in accordance with the money they possessed or could borrow or steal—even at the moment when the crosswalks teemed with harried sales-clerks rushing tardily back to work and money men strolling calmly in their opulent overcoats to what they assured one another were their indispensable professions, while swarms of Christmas shoppers, the season's annual visitors, having stripped bare the shelves and display cases of the downtown shops, lined the curbs and howled for taxis—even, for that matter, while the great bells in the dingy downtown churches rested after their noon peals and gathered strength for the Advent evening's Angelus, and the loud taxis roared by unstopping, indifferent to the sidewalks dense with shivering people poking at their cell phones for an Uber ride, and the Salvation Army's Santas furiously ringing hand bells above their red donation kettles, and the anxious delivery trucks beeping in a discordant choir as they tried to back into loading zones, like some madman's electronic attempt to render "The Carol of the Bells" in the most irrelevant and irreverent tones he could find; in short, even as all the visible world had become a bustling Christmas cityscape straight out of a Charles Dickens story—even then, Bart Sagan sat unmoving on the window seat and stared out at the snowy, busy scene below him.

Three days he had remained there inside his apartment, disregarding the increasingly frantic phone calls and poundings at the door. Three days with nothing gained since he had taken the packages from Michael Stuyvesant and Cicely D'Angelo, with Harry King's deadline—and the probability that the white and gold gift boxes would be opened at Christmas—falling down on him like an avalanche.

Not that the days had been entirely wasted, although Bart wouldn't know that until finally, early on December 23rd, the fourth morning since his robberies began, he stirred himself—bundling up and heading out into the cold to begin work. And it was down on the corner of State and Main, within sight of Harry King's building, that Bart noticed Toby Veck and his daughter Meg, con artists with whom he and Liz sometimes worked, brushing past the hardcase stick-up man Caleb Plummer and giving him the wink.

Curious to see what could bring the dissimilar criminals together, Bart turned up his collar, pulled down his hat, and settled into a cautious shadow, following them up State Street toward the cathedral. Following them, in fact, till they came to a modern-looking apartment building, one of the addresses—just to be sure, Bart ducked behind a Santa and reindeer display and checked his copy of the list—to which a heroin package had been sent.

In itself, that was enough of a coincidence to set Bart worrying. But then he saw Meg and Caleb take up the places of yet more criminals he recognized: the pickpocket May Fielding and the safecracker Will Fern, who casually slipped Toby their notebooks and strolled off arm in arm, approximating as best they could an innocent pair of Christmas shoppers. Toby nodded to his daughter and the armed robber, pocketed the previous watchers' notebooks, and strolled off himself, turning east on Third.

It took Bart over an hour to piece together the operation, and he found himself inordinately proud that he had lost the wary Toby only once—when, after making a call from a pay phone, the old man had suddenly stepped out into the street to hail a taxi and speed off, while Bart argued vainly with a woman, her arms full of Christmas packages, who claimed the taxi he had frantically managed to stop. But Bart picked up Toby again when, finding at last another cab, he made a guess and directed the driver to the nearest unvisited address on the shipping company's list.

By the time Toby turned on High Street, hunching his shoulders against the wind, and disappeared into the Evergreen Tavern, Bart had watched him make five stops—visiting, like a policeman's bad dream, as odd a collection of the city's criminals as anyone could imagine. Professor Redlaw, the con man, and the hulking Tetterby brothers (even though Bart was sure he'd heard they were still in jail for everything from attempted murder to aggravated jaywalking). The get-away drivers Milly and Bill Swidger. The pencil-thin fence Ben Britain, of all people, and Clemency Newcome, who had decided long ago never to live up to the name with which her hopeful parents had baptized her. Even blond and blue-eyed Michael Warden, the widow's friend, of whom the best that could be said was that he might not rob an orphanage if he already had some money in his pocket.

Bart hesitated a surprisingly long time in the vestibule of a used-clothing store down the street, pretending to examine the window display of dated ties, dusty costume jewelry, and the corpses of last summer's flies—a cheap glass necklace blinking at him in the angled morning light. It wasn't fear that made him pause, he decided. It was more a desire *not* to know, *not* to be drawn into, whatever his friends and business acquaintances had gotten themselves up to. He already lacked a plan for deflecting

Harry King's threats against the town's minor criminals, and here were those same criminals running around in some crazy effort to make things more complicated.

But he knew, of course, that he had to face up to it, and so at last, with a sigh, his hand on his hat to keep it from blowing away, Bart walked up the block and opened the tavern door—only to be hit by a wave of noise that nearly knocked him back out again into High Street.

There was Gruff Tackleton, a giant goat of a man, shouting across the room while he kept watch on the door. Snitchy and Craggs. Arthur Heathfield. Dr. Jeddler, the sometime surgeon, who would fix up a bullet wound if he were sober enough to see it. Sitting at the bar, having taken over the daily-specials blackboard, was Bart's accountant, the long, thin, pale Mr. Filer, preparer of fraudulent tax returns for most of town's underworld. No one knew his first name, and legend had it that he never left his office—sleeping on the couch and cooking his meals on a hot plate out of fear the IRS would slip in and bug the place while he was gone. But here he was at the Evergreen, marking down times and places in yellow chalk.

"Bart!" shouted Dot Perrybingle from the table where she sat with her slow, lumbering brother John, and like a wave in a stadium the word spread across the tavern. Mad Tilly, tying small, precise knots in a piece of string. Dangerous Joe Bowley. The party girls and occasional burglars Grace and Marion. Thieves and grifters and prowlers; pickpockets, pilferers, and scroungers; housebreakers, heisters, and hijackers. Everyone from highway robbers to shoplifters seemed to be gathered, a larcenous assembly of the town's crooks. And perched there at the center, as proud as a catbird, was his friend Liz McCally.

"Oh, Bart," she cried. "What took you so long?"

"A Tom and Jerry for each of you," Tim the bartender announced, setting down a pair of foaming Christmas mugs, red with white snowflakes, as Bart sat at Liz's table with all the calm confidence of a man who suspects his chair is wired with explosives and wants to shoot the people responsible.

"Dancing Dan brought in his special recipe. Everybody here has been drinking them, the past few days, while they've been . . . um"—he flinched away from Liz's glare—"doing whatever it is they've been doing. I don't ask questions." Turning away and striding across the room, he added in a loud voice, "Hey, guys, can you keep it down to a dull roar? The sweethearts need to talk."

Bart stared down at his hot drink, sprinkled with nutmeg. He glanced up at the Christmas decorations and gazed around the crowded bar. He turned his head sideways to examine the notebooks from which Liz had been typing information into her laptop computer. He even swiveled to study the tables to the left, to the right, in front, at his back, and only then— as the noise of the establishment gradually lessened—did he meet the eyes of the pretty, apprehensive face across the table and ask, in the most reasonable tone he could manage, "What in God's name have you done, Liz?"

"It . . . well, it got a little out of control, maybe," she answered. "But really," she added, gaining speed, "all this is your fault. Okay, I made some phone calls, and everybody I talked to wanted to pitch in. And then *they* made phone calls, and, yeah, the people they called made even more phone calls, and by the end of the first night I had more help than I knew what to do with, and the word was still spreading. You disappeared for days, my friend Johnny called me from Minnesota screaming for advice about the job *you* sent him on, and nobody has a clue how to stop Harry King. So what was I supposed to do?"

She was sputtering by this point, her anxiety having transmuted by some arcane alchemy into anger. "Days," Liz repeated. "Days, without a word. Days, without telling me what I should be doing. So, I . . . I," she faltered, glancing around and noticing as if for the first time how full the tavern had become. "I guess I kind of organized things."

But as Bart opened his mouth to speak, she started up again. "Anyway, what right do you have to criticize? If you can't be responsible, Bart, then someone else has to be. Besides"—and her tone grew more wheedling— "we've already found where all the packages are here in town. And Johnny's closing in on the one in Minnesota." Liz paused for a moment. "Well, *probably* closing in."

She held up a finger to stop Bart from interrupting while she gulped at her drink. "There's plenty more," she added in a rush. "We've got every local place under surveillance, with notes about the residents and alarm systems and even blueprints, where we could find them, everything written down. Plus Harry King's place. Billy Euston has been helping with that. You remember: King's nephew in-law or something, the guy who lost the drugs. He came in here the other day, looking for you, so I put him to work. Mr. Filer has been keeping the watch schedules, and Professor Redlaw conned a clerk down at city hall for sewer maps, in case we need them, and everybody has been pitching in, even though it's Christmastime."

Liz took another swallow. "But finding the packages, that's the main thing. And I managed to keep everybody in check, just like you said—even though they were all pushing me to start swapping out the drugs. Oh, and we've bought some good wine, a pair of bottles weighing exactly enough. After that, I wanted to send them home, but I couldn't, because it's, like, Christmas with one another, you know? Everybody was being so helpful, and we were working together as a team, and you were missing, and I didn't have a plan. They all want some way to pull Harry King down, but nobody can figure out anything except to get the packages and give him what he wants, and it's driving them crazy. Crazy," she said with a choking laugh. "Crazy."

"They hate King that much?" asked Bart, finally getting in a word.

"You idiot," she shouted, the whole tavern falling quiet and turning to look. "They didn't come just to get Harry King. They came to help *you*."

"How long since you slept?" Bart asked Liz gently in the ensuing silence.

"I don't know. A couple days. Things just kind of snowballed, and I had to keep on top of them. I mean, it's December 23rd already, and we've got nothing."

"No," Bart answered. "I managed to lift two of the packages, the ones out in the suburbs. So you can call off your watchers there. For the rest, what do we have? Schedules of deliveries? A list of the different locks? Notes on who has access?"

"Everything," Liz replied, sitting up as she watched Bart look around the room as though weighing up the strengths and weaknesses surrounding them. "We have everything anybody could find out over three days, which"—she gestured down at the pile of notebooks—"turns out to be a lot."

Bart glanced around the room again. "You don't even like half these people, Liz," he said quietly.

"Yeah, well, they're criminals. What do you expect? But they're all their own criminals, if that makes any sense. They aren't sneaks, and they don't belong to Harry King. Well, except maybe for Billy Euston. I can't figure out what he's doing here, day after day, moping around, waiting for you like you're some kind of sage who's going to fill him with ancient wisdom. But all I've said is that we're working on what his boss demanded, so what else can he report back to King? I mean, that *is* what we're doing, isn't it? Obeying Harry King's orders? Unless you've got a plan I don't know about."

But Bart didn't answer, looking over instead at the miserable kid hunched in the corner—really looking, seeing for the first time his unhappiness and resentment, his hunger for something more. Then Bart's fingers began to move on the table, as though he were playing unconscious scales on an invisible piano, and he raised his eyes to focus for a long moment on some distant horizon.

"Bart?" Liz called. "Bart? *BART?* Are you listening?"

"Hmm?" he answered, coming back to her.

"I asked if you have a plan."

He met her eyes and smiled for the first time in days. "I think I might, sweetheart. I think I just might."

Bart took a swallow from his Tom and Jerry. "You know, Tim was right," he said, like a food critic taking time from a busy schedule to savor a morsel. "These are good. Not a breakfast drink exactly, but we have to get Dan's recipe."

"As God is my witness," the red-eyed Liz hissed, "if you don't tell me, I'm going to shoot you and have everyone here testify it was justifiable homicide."

"I can't explain all of it. Not yet. Let me keep one surprise, just in case things go bad," Bart explained. "But here's how it starts. I need to have a talk with Billy. Maybe do a little shopping for supplies this morning. Then we'll hit all of the remaining places either this afternoon or tonight. Nine jobs in a row. This is going to be epic."

He pulled over one of the notebooks, tore out a sheet, and started jotting down notes. "In the meantime, I need you to put together a schedule for the hits. Which ones in daylight? Which ones at night? Cons or sneak-ins? No strong-arm if you can help it, but one way or another, they all have to be done long before daybreak. By midnight, if we possibly can."

He underlined something on the page. "Get a few people to help you lay it out. Redlaw, maybe. And Mr. Filer, since he's here. Meg Veck, too: Time for her to learn how to step up, whatever her father says."

He studied his notes for a moment and added, "You'll need one of the real burglars in on the planning, as well. Heathfield, I guess; he's the best of them. Assign a hardcase or two to each job as backup and protection, but don't let them take the lead. We want these to go quietly. Make Gruff Tackleton part of your inner group and use him to keep the tough guys in line; he's a pro and knows how it works."

Bart made one last note, circled something, and laughed as he looked down at the paper. "And there we are. Set up the jobs so I can join as many as possible, one after another." He laughed again, returning to the high-energy Bart that Liz had always known before. "A kind of rolling hit. A Christmas crime spree. Look at it this way, Liz: We're going to do a reverse Santa Claus—taking something from everyone on our list, whether they've been naughty or nice."

He stood up and called across the tavern, "Billy, will you take a walk with me outside? I've got a story I want to tell you." Then he turned back to the table and took a final swallow from his drink. "You know," he repeated in a wondering tone. "These are *really* good. I'll call you by noon, one o'clock at the latest, and tell you if it's on for today."

Then Bart Sagan, the thief, leaned down and kissed Liz McCally the grifter on the top her head. "Thanks, sweetheart, for everything. You've saved us all," he whispered. And in a swirl of motion, he made his way across the room—smiling, touching shoulders, greeting the town's criminals. Gathering up the battered drug-runner Billy Euston. And sweeping out the door into the cold wind of High Street.

V

It ends . . . but then, these kinds of stories don't end. Not really. They only flicker from time to time with small epiphanies and revelations, like the falling of a curtain across the stage to signal a break: the completion of one particular act in the long human comedy.

Think of it as the conclusion of a chapter rather than the closing of a book. The wealthy but ill Michael Stuyvesant, for instance—where will his curtain fall? The panic-stricken Johnny Jasper, off in Minnesota, for that matter? And Harry King, the drug lord, and that obsequious jeweler who sold him a hundred-thousand-dollar necklace for his wife, sliding like starlight through Mr. King's thick hands? Cicely D'Angelo, dreaming in her chair. The bruiser Gruff Tackleton. The sneak-thieves Snitchy and Craggs. Everyone has a different arc. Everyone comes to a different end.

But since this is Bart's story, more or less, we should probably leave the tale where he set it down—on a table at the Evergreen Tavern on Christmas Eve, wrapped neatly in red paper with a white bow: a small Christmas present, waiting for Liz McCally to arrive.

Of course, to reach that point, the town's criminals had to retrieve nine of the twelve packages in a single day, and the rolling Christmas crimes began only around two in the afternoon, when Bart finally telephoned to tell Liz the campaign was on.

The details are still a little unclear. Everyone agrees that, in the rush, Mr. Filer emerged as the point man: the cadaverous accountant in a prim dark suit, balanced on a bar stool as he tracked the jobs, quickly becoming the only one with the whole picture. But since he was also the kind of man who wouldn't tell a nun whether it was raining—wouldn't tell her mother superior and a choir of angels, as far as that goes—no one has ever heard his account of the day's events. Bart stayed in the field, Liz was too antsy not to rush out to join him, and everyone else had only a partial view of how things unfolded. The Evergreen's bartender Tim sometimes talks about it, gassing away to regulars on a slow evening, but it's hard to say what portion of his version is myth, lathered on like frosting, and what portion really happened.

Anyway, as the story goes, only one of the jobs broke down into the kind of strong-arm robbery that both Bart and Mr. King wanted to avoid. That package was being held, for an out-of-town tenant, behind the concierge desk of an upscale and surprisingly scam-proof apartment building. After two failed cons (a mailman gag and then an impromptu try by Liz, spilling things from her purse while she asked for directions), the Tetterby brothers had had enough. With a growl, they squeezed out of the watchers' car, marched in, slammed the officious clerk down against the desk when he objected, grabbed the brown-paper-wrapped Christmas box out of the mail room behind the desk, and marched out again—a single Tetterby finger, pointed menacingly, enough to freeze in place everyone else in the building's lobby.

That was one of the drug packages that didn't get replaced with Liz's wine bottles. Other addresses, however, proved more amenable. Two, for example, were straight-forward daylight slip-ins—a quiet picking of back-door locks while the houses' residents were out. Find the boxes (one under a tree, the other unwrapped on an entry table), make the substitutions, and relock the doors: in and out, as graceful as dancers. Will Fern and May Fielding paired up for those jobs.

Professor Redlaw's charts of the storm-sewer lines never did get used. There seems to have been a plan to follow them to an access hatch in the basement of another apartment building, but when the burglary team arrived, they discovered a fire door that hadn't latched and decided they might as well keep their clothes clean.

Unfortunately, once inside, they found the white Christmas box not only unpacked but opened: the tape-wrapped bag of drugs sitting out on the kitchen counter with a yellow sticky note that read, "Bob—Is this supposed to be some kind of joke?" After a series of increasingly acrimonious phone calls, the drunk Dr. Jeddler came up with the answer, shouting it across the tavern to Mr. Filer. So Dot Perrybingle and her brother John carefully slit the package, emptied its heroin into a trash bag, and refilled it with flour, sugar, and baking soda they borrowed from the cupboards. A little wiping up and hiding of the evidence, some re-taping of the package, and the Perrybingles left the apartment pretty much as they had found it—minus, of course, the heroin, a green plastic trash bag, and 6.6 pounds of baking supplies.

As for the swaps accomplished by the con artists, the first was in a house with a for-sale sign in the snow on the front yard. A visit to the realtor by Grace and the handsome Michael Warden cracked that one open as easy an egg. Joe Bowley and the grim Clemency Newcome took the two in run-down apartments down by the river—posing as city inspectors on a hunt for violations and bulldozing the building managers into a cooperative frame of mind. The biggest scam involved a fake city-services crew, a real gas leak that started to get out of control, and a 911 call that brought three fire trucks, two police cars, and an ambulance screaming up the icy streets. A half-dozen con artists it took to create that little masterpiece of overkill, leaving three houses evacuated and two fistfights started before they finally managed to slip away with the drugs.

And then there was the last job: a good, old-fashioned, not-a-creature-was-stirring burglary, the family asleep in their beds. Bart and Arthur Heathfield took that one. As Tim the bartender tells the story, a little girl caught them, padding down the stairs in her nightgown to ask what they were doing under the tree. To which, naturally, they answered that they were Santa's helpers, gave her a glass of milk, and sent her back up the stairs to bed. But not even the tavern's regulars believe him. Some stories are too much like stories to be true.

Still, this much is certain: It was just after midnight—a few minutes into Christmas Eve Day—that Bart rose to thank the criminals reconvened at the Evergreen. One green trash bag and ten clear plastic packages of heroin safe in the trunk of his car, and nine jobs pulled off in a single day: a heroic, almost miraculous endeavor.

"Marion," he asked, reaching down and gently tugging from Mad Tilly's neat fingers the piece of origami she was folding from one of the stray notebooks pages, "will you and Mr. Filer make sure all this paper gets burned or shredded? As for the rest of you, if you stop by after 5:00 in the afternoon, there will be Christmas presents here for everybody." Liz made a noise to interrupt, but Bart overrode her. "I know, I know. None of you did this for pay. But I'm grateful—grateful beyond words—so let me try to express my gratitude with a thank-you gift."

"Man, these are good," he added, sipping at his last Tom and Jerry of the day. "Dan, send me the recipe, and I swear I'll add a little extra, just for you." He put a hand on Tilly's shoulder and said, "Meanwhile, I've got one or two more jobs to do tonight. Some presents to fix up. Tilly, you're good at wrapping things. Will you help me? Everyone else, thank you again. Thank you."

Gesturing to Billy Euston to join them, Bart shrugged into his overcoat and made his way to the door. "Oh, and one last thing," he called back. "Sleep in tomorrow, Liz. You've done enough for all of us."

And while the criminals cheered her, Bart and his companions left the warm tavern and ventured out in the cold Christmas Eve morning, following the illumination of a distant streetlight to his car.

"Did you hear the news?" the bartender Tim called out as Liz came through the door of the Evergreen Tavern on Christmas Eve, a little before 5:00 in the afternoon.

"No," she answered with a smile. "What news? I haven't heard a thing." In fact, Liz had slept late—very late—that morning, reveling in what seemed her first peaceful rest in ages. And then, resolutely refusing to check her messages or answer her phone, she'd spent the remainder of the day in a happy haze: puttering around her apartment, doing small chores, wrapping presents, humming softly to herself.

"Oh, nothing much," Tim said, in his element as purveyor of drinks and the latest word. "Just that Bart is on the run, Harry King is in jail, the police chief is on a rampage, and half the town has gone crazy. Gunfights, I hear, down by the river. Some Yuletide we're having, isn't it?"

"Bart's on the run?" Liz repeated bewilderedly. "Wait, what are you talking about? I don't . . . I mean . . . King's in jail? Where's Bart?"

"That's what I'm trying to tell you," said Tim, and, in his account, it all begins earlier that day, when Harry King gives his wife a present in front of his guests at an afternoon Christmas reception. Rich food, a string quartet, an open bar, unctuous speeches about King's past innocence but future promises not to sully himself "by association with those less concerned" than King "with a moral appearance and the city's good name." And then the gift giving, starting with the announcement of a large charitable donation to the city's cultural foundations and ending with a present for King's wife.

Which she unwraps, to the continuation of general applause, and reveals as a velvet-covered jewelry case. A jewelry case, as it happens, that looks as though it's leaking dust. And when she snaps it open on its spring hinges, it jumps in her hands, spraying fine white powder over herself and several of the women near her—one of them the city council's representative for district three. It's in their hair, down their cleavage, on their hands: a mess that makes them look like the powdered ghosts of eighteenth-century French courtiers, come back as the revenge of Louis XVI.

Well, the string quartet falls silent, the guests freeze, Harry King is ready to explode, and nobody knows what to do. Nobody, that is, but the district attorney's recent bride—beautiful, greedy, and empty-headed beyond even the town's usual standard for rich men's third wives—who has taken the opportunity to open the neat wrapping of her own gift box.

"Oh," she cries into the silence, and every head turns toward her. "What are we supposed to use this for? Is it expensive?"

Very expensive, as things turn out, for what she's holding up in her pretty hands for all to see is a taped-up plastic package, filled with white powder and weighing, at a guess, around 6.6 pounds.

Now others in the room start opening their boxes to find similar gifts. The white-powdered councilwoman meets the eye of a senior police official, who nods and uses his pocket knife to cut a small hole in his own package. Touching a tiny portion to his tongue, he spits and starts beckoning wildly for his aide, the young policeman who accompanied him to the party.

And that was pretty much that. Oh, there were still scenes to be played out: Harry King's bellowing, and his own associates' deciding maybe discretion was the better choice, quietly wiping their fingerprints off their guns and hiding them under the linen tablecloths as the police came charging through the door. Paramedics summoned to keep the heroin-dusted women from getting drug poisoning. Loud demands from the mayor to be told what was going on.

But really, everything was determined, the whole drama moving toward its predictable end, from the moment Mrs. King opened the case of what was supposed to be a diamond necklace from her husband. As the police took statements and gathered evidence, Harry King, lord of all he could see, was led from the room in handcuffs. Not, however, before having a whispered but heated conference with his lawyer, in which—rumor among the town's criminals insisted—the name of Bart Sagan was repeated several times.

Liz McCally lowered herself slowly onto the seat of a back booth—the same booth in which had she sat, six days before, to hear the story of Billy Euston's blunder and Harry King's threats. Bart had come by the tavern, oh, must have been around 1:00, the bartender had said, leaving some things for her and promising to call just after 5:00.

What she found in the booth were a set of thick white envelopes, two dozen or so, lined up between the salt and pepper shakers. Baskets on the opposite bench overflowing like Santa's bag with jars of caviar and truffles—Sumatran coffee at $400 a pound and expensive bottles of wine. And there on the table, in front of the spot in which she had sat at their earlier meeting, was a small Christmas package with her name on it, wrapped in red and white.

Avoiding touching the present, avoiding even thinking about it, Liz pulled out one of the envelopes and saw on the front Gruff Tackleton's name in Bart's clear handwriting. Unsealed, of course; he's always too trusting, she thought angrily, deflecting the impulse to cry before it overwhelmed her. Too trusting in too many ways, even while he didn't trust her enough to let her in on the plan to get King—to let *her*, his one real friend, help. Mad Tilly and that stupid kid Billy were the people Bart took with him when he left the Evergreen, the ones who must have been with him when he broke into King's offices and planted the drugs.

Inside the envelope she found a half-inch of currency, all hundred-dollar bills: maybe $10,000. Assuming an envelope for everyone who had joined in the jobs the day before, that came to around a quarter of a million dollars, just lying there on the table, waiting for Liz to distribute it.

She was finally reaching for the small Christmas present—reaching for it, pulling back as though it had burned her, and then reaching for it again—when her cell phone rang.

"Hello, Bart," she answered it quietly, at last lifting up the package with her other hand and reading the simple "For Elizabeth Ann McCally" on the label. "Why'd you do it? Why didn't you tell me?"

"I wanted to protect you," he replied in a soothing voice. "King is probably going to be too busy to do much in the way of revenge, but this way, if he does go after anyone, it'll be just me and not you. Not any of the other independents." Bart laughed. "Besides, how's he going to beat a drug rap when he doused some of this city's most respectable people with heroin? I hear they're going to hit him with a dozen charges of attempted murder, on top of possession and trafficking. Meanwhile, every would-be gangster in town is out grabbing a piece of his empire, now that Billy has tipped them off."

"Yeah, Billy," said Liz tonelessly. "Why did you take him with you last night? And poor, crazy Tilly, too?"

"Ah," Bart answered. "You mean, why didn't I take you? I needed Billy to help get me into King's penthouse, guide me through me the layout. And I wanted Tilly because she's the neatest person I know, and we needed to unwrap the presents, pack them with the drugs, and then wrap them again exactly enough that none of King's people would notice they'd been tampered with. I didn't take you because you were exhausted, and because . . . well, because I didn't want you to get caught with me, if something went wrong."

Liz felt her tears starting to rise again and began to open her present as carefully as she could, preserving the paper and bow just to show Bart—or herself, at least—that she was every bit as neat as Tilly. "And all these envelopes?" she asked. "I'm supposed to just hand them out? How can you afford it?"

"Yeah, the envelopes. Filling them cleaned out my emergency get-away fund. Every penny I could lay my hands on, in fact. But I, ah"—Bart laughed again—"I managed to do a little replenishing. You remember when I told you that King said he had to give the bigwigs some quiet money? Well, Billy had overheard the exact amounts. So, while Billy kept watch at the door and Tilly rewrapped the presents, I sat down at King's desk and booted up his computer. Easiest work I've ever done. All I had to do was use the amounts of his last large withdrawals to get online access to his main account."

There was a long crackle of static on the line, as though Bart were going through a tunnel, before he continued, "From there I could reach out to all his other accounts. The Cayman Islands, Europe, here in the city. I cleaned him out, Liz. He kept all his information in that one computer, and I transferred his money to banks scattered around the world. He's never getting it back. This is a big one, Liz. Even after helping Billy set himself up, it's enough cash to last me a good long stretch."

She could almost hear Bart smiling. "By the way," he added, "did you ever hear any news from Minnesota?"

"Just a message from Johnny yesterday morning, saying he was still working on it." Liz had finally peeled off the wrapping paper, revealing a small blue box. "Where are you now?" she asked quietly.

"About a hundred, a hundred and fifty, miles away," Bart answered. "I figured the airport might be watched, so I'm driving to the coast. Then I thought I'd catch a plane out of the country, till things cool down. Tokyo, maybe, or Singapore. Busan. Out on the Pacific Rim, anyway. You knew I grew up out there, didn't you? My grandparents were missionaries, and . . . I don't know, I just started to feel that maybe it was time to go visit for a while. Time to head back to the Far East and get things straight."

Liz lifted off the top of the box and found under the cotton batting a cheap glass-bead necklace, with a price tag still attached from the used-clothing store a few doors down High Street. "And what's this?" she asked. "This $12.40 piece of costume jewelry you've given me for Christmas?"

"It's not jewelry, exactly," he answered, fading as though into the distance. "It's more like a promise. A promise I'll come back." As the cell-phone service dropped the line, replacing Bart Sagan's voice with a dull buzz, Liz McCally lifted the necklace up to the light, where it danced and glittered against the old, polished wood of the Evergreen Tavern's ceiling.

And that's the end of this particular story, the falling of its curtain— except perhaps for one final note. After church on Christmas morning, after the annual phone calls with her great-nieces and nephews, scattered across the country, Cicely D'Angelo laid out for herself in the front room a pot of tea and a plate of cookies from a round blue tin. Perched on her chair, she gazed fondly at the new pairs of animals she had set near her crèche— each of them being greeted, she imagined, by their older companions in the long procession to pay homage to the Holy Infant in a manger. This year's Christmas gifts, sent by her young students, of course. Or, rather, not so young. Grown old now themselves, she had to admit, although in memory they still lived as the girls and boys they had been. Such promise, such hope: new lights just beginning to shine.

She dozed off for a moment, or perhaps she merely slipped into her reminiscences, hardly distinguishable from dreams. But returning gently to the waking world, she found her eyes focused on the white box beneath the tree, left by that clever and dangerous young man who had come to visit. The poor child with a terrible puzzle to solve.

Clearing away the tea dishes and washing up, Cicely hummed an old dance tune—not terribly Christmasy, she smiled to think, but that's all right, just this once. Back in the front room, the white box in her lap, she lifted the lid to see whether the thief had left her anything when he slipped out, believing her asleep. And in wonder, from the depths of tissue paper, she brought out a brilliant silver necklace, gems flowing like starlight in her tiny hands. Terribly expensive, it must be, she could see, and much too fine to wear, of course. But then, young men are often foolish that way. Such a lovely boy.

With a sigh, setting the box on the floor, she rose from her chair to set the necklace on the table with her animals, as though it were yet another little gift from yet another student—weaving it carefully around the crèche to lie at the feet of Mary as the Wise Men and shepherds approached the manger. Yes, she decided, that's where it goes: there among the Christmas things.

Nativity

I

Michael Stuyvesant came from money. A quiet family wealth had made and formed him, fashioning him from the womb. Nothing ostentatious or flamboyant. Nothing that called too much attention to itself. Just the well-chosen nannies and the suitable schools, the proper clothing and the appropriate church—a creaky but still effective old American blueblood system designed to weigh him, evaluate his talents, put him to the correct use, and ensure that he delivered the family estate intact to the next generation of Stuyvesants.

He might have been a senior political wise man, gently advising presidents and secretaries of state, had the system judged him so. He might have slipped into upper-level management, as his children would later do, sitting on the boards of stable banks and long-settled businesses. He might have become a superior Episcopal clergyman, dean of the nearby cathedral or bishop even, if the call to that vocation had come.

Instead, he settled for being a competent if somewhat distant and ironical lawyer, occupying himself by lending his family name to a local law firm and navigating for his clients the complexities of the federal tax code. The cool, efficient system had brought him through childhood with no major dings or bruises, seen him well married, and helped him establish his own son and daughter in their own busy careers. And now, with the return of his pancreatic cancer at age sixty-four, the system was providing its final service: ushering him gracefully down to the grave.

Or as gracefully, anyway, as it could manage when, on December 20 at around 4:00 in the afternoon—127 miles southwest of Minneapolis,

Minnesota, and half a continent from home—Michael Stuyvesant found himself standing over the passed-out body of a drunken Santa Claus in the middle of the worst snowstorm he could remember, with a pregnant teenager screeching at him from the open door of his rental car and the messy wet flakes caught in mid-air by the yellow-orange blink of the hazard lights: sudden revelations, strange illuminations, of the world's disorder.

II

Even before the car service came to carry him to the airport for his trip, Michael Stuyvesant suspected he was making a mistake. Last-minute travels and unplanned visits were not unknown in the family. His older cousin Amy was famous for descending on her relatives unannounced—trailing caravans of luggage, the latest of her handsome young friends, and a cloud of smoke from the cigars she affected. Nieces and nephews would stop over unexpectedly on their drives up to college or down to the beaches for spring break, needing a bed. But greater decorum was generally expected of the more settled members of the family: a longer period of notice; a politer, more stately sense of time. His son and daughter, and their families, would be startled, even disturbed, to see him in Denver for Christmas, only two months before they were all scheduled to meet on a skiing trip to Switzerland.

The trouble was that he did not know how he would be feeling by February. Not well, he imagined, with his doctors predicting no more than six months left to him. And he could not bring himself to tell his children over the phone. Oh, getting documents signed, making arrangements—those were ostensible reasons for the sudden trip. But really, he knew, it boiled down to sentimentality. He simply felt unable to blurt it out to their disembodied presence down a telephone line, and the truth was he wanted to *see* them, visit with his grandchildren, one more time while he was still feeling reasonably strong and stable. At the end, he suspected, he would want mostly to be alone.

So he packed with precision a small suitcase. Or rather, since he had always been a precise man in life's little things, he now packed with even more precision than usual, squaring the corners of his pressed shirts and boxer shorts as he set them, just so, in the brown leather case. Interesting, he thought, how dying concentrates the mind. Of course, as the old joke ran, there is not much gain from it—since what dying concentrates the mind on is mostly the fact that one is dying.

But even that was not entirely true. He watched his hands, his long always-clever fingers, fastening the buckles of the suitcase with a kind of quick, controlled exactitude, and he understood that such motions seemed fascinating only because they were to be repeated so few times before . . . before . . . before the end. He paused and leaned in exhaustion over the suitcase for a moment, cursing himself. The cancer had physically weakened him, he knew, and the ineffective medicines had drained another portion of his strength, but that should not have been enough to make him weak in mind as well. To make him tremble like this. He had known since he was a child that he would die. He had been reared by that long tradition of his American blueblood family to tell no lies and fear no future. And now he lacked the simple strength to face his own death with the equanimity and confidence of his ancestors.

He arose, and went for his life, and came to Beersheba. . . . And he sat down under a juniper tree . . . and said, "It is enough; now, O Lord, take away my life; for I am not better than my fathers." Where was that from? The Book of Kings, probably. The prophet Elijah fleeing the wrath of Jezebel. Ah, well, he thought with a half smile of self-mockery, I am no prophet, and I doubt an angel will come to me. Michael rose and went down the stairs to eat a little something before the car came, listening to the voices of his housekeeper and gardener squabbling in the pantry.

In the event, the trip west proved smooth, at least at the start: the car to the regional airport, and there, waiting for him, the small jet whose time his secretary had rented from a consortium of his less-respectable clients—including Harry King, the reputed drug lord, whose accountants had recently approached him for tax advice. Michael had planned to turn King's people down, not wanting to touch that soiled wealth, and since he was paying for the jet's time, he did not feel he owed them any favor.

Besides, he observed grimly, he was not likely to be around long enough for them to insist. Michael ran his finger along the pampered arm of soft leather on his seat as the plane trundled down the runway. So much of what passes for opulence in this country, he thought, bears little relation to what rich people know or even want. America constructs even its extravagances from lower-class fantasies—the picture people had of what their ordinary lives would be if they could live them with unlimited money: comfort over beauty, ostentation over taste, newness over inheritance. The aesthetics of Harry King and all his ilk, overrunning the world.

Ah, well, he thought, that seems the price of getting out and doing something. How Ann would have loved this. She had always pushed him to be more impulsive. Rent a plane, pay an unexpected visit. Just what she would have ordered if . . . if . . . Michael winced. Unsurprising to think of her now, he realized—to feel a hard twinge of grief. He really was weakening, and even the wall behind which he kept the pain of her car wreck, ten years ago, was thinning and growing fragile. The flight attendant brought Michael Stuyvesant a drink, and he watched in dull vagueness the checkerboard of cold December fields slide by beneath the plane—until the co-pilot emerged from the cockpit with a worried look on his face.

"We, um, we have a problem, sir," the tall cadaverous man began, nervously rubbing his hands. Evidently Harry King had made clear to his employees how he felt about excuses. "The, ah, the storm we saw pushing up from the southwest has picked up a lot more speed than the weather service predicted, and we have to . . . I mean, the towers are ordering us to divert. Minneapolis is, um, the best we can manage. They won't let us go further west right now, and after we land, within a few hours, the, ah, storm is predicted to sweep in and drop record snow."

The co-pilot swallowed, the Adam's apple on his scrawny throat bobbing in mute anxiety. "I'm sorry, sir. When we left, we should have had enough to time to make it all the way to Denver, but it's like a freak supernatural occurrence or something. The storm barreled northeast faster than anything we've ever seen, and once it hit the cold front coming down from Canada it . . . it just caught us, I guess. The big commercial planes—the tower will start moving them out in about twelve hours. Or even twenty-four. Private planes like us, we won't be cleared for at least another six hours. Maybe more. I'm really sorry, sir, but there's nothing we can do. Nothing, really."

A stick figure, Michael thought, staring at the man: a stick figure out of Charles Dickens's novels, rubbing his hands like a nervous waiter. Every time Michael went out in the world, he discovered that Dickens had never written fiction; he had merely described people the way they actually are. "Well, then," he answered coldly, "we will have to go to Minneapolis. If we arrive there soon enough, perhaps I can rent a car and drive the northern route, staying enough ahead of the storm to make it through. Please radio ahead to have a car waiting for me. Have them call my secretary to settle the arrangements. And thank you," he added, his careful courtesy, another gift of his upbringing, returning to him, "for letting me know. I understand that you do not control the paths of the storm."

III

"I'm Cheyenne," said the girl. "Cheyenne from Minnesota, and I'm going to Cheyenne in Wyoming. Isn't that too funny? Cheyenne to Cheyenne, and she ain't no Shy Ann. Horses shy, too, when they run away. I read that once, in a book called *Misty*. *Misty of Chincoteague.* Do you know it? For ages and ages, almost the whole year I was fourteen, I made everyone call me Misty, like the horse. But now I'm Cheyenne, like the city. And the river, too. And a mountain and an Indian tribe. I looked it up."

She turned in the seat of the black Hummer SUV to look at the driver as he negotiated his way out of the airport toward Highway 169, following the driving instructions of the GPS mounted on the dash. The sky was gray and darkening in the early afternoon, but no snow had fallen yet. The machine, he decided, handled more like a boat than a car. He had not driven anything this big since the old land yachts, the Lincolns and the Cadillacs and the Chrysler Imperials, of the 1960s. Another loss of elegance: from luxury cars designed to show off Jack and Jackie Kennedy's good looks, to luxury cars whose blueprints came from an armored military vehicle.

"You're awfully quiet," the small girl said. "If we're going to ride together all the way to Wyoming, I guess I should know your name, too. I mean, they know who you are back at the airport, I'm sure, so if you were like a serial killer or something, the police could find out who took me. But you don't look like one. A serial killer, I mean. Though I never met a serial killer. Not a real one. Just the ones in the movies. Did you?"

He grunted in amusement. "Stuyvesant. Michael Stuyvesant," he answered. "And no, I have never met a serial killer. Not, as you say, a real one."

"Ah, that's a nice name. You could change it, though, if you wanted. I've changed mine dozens of times. But now I'm Cheyenne. Oh," she stopped, her hand to her mouth, "I already said that. Anyways, Michael Driving-to-Denver-and-Dropping-Me-off-in-Cheyenne Stuyvesant, I just wanted to say that I'm glad you offered me a ride, but you didn't have to rescue me. The guy at the terminal, the private-jet place where you landed: I could have handled him. He was just a would-be wolf, like any other guy, who maybe had some fantasy about making it with a pregnant girl. I could have sweet-talked him into letting me stay until the flights started again, dodged a few clumsy kisses, pretended I had morning sickness—you know, the whole bag of tricks that girls on the road learn."

Michael was silent for a moment, watching the gray road unfurl before him down through the Minnesota hills. However breezily the girl talked, he had seen the fat, sweaty man at the counter, the sole employee left as the storm swept in, holding her wrists as she tried to pull away. A tiny girl, maybe five-one or -two, and a teenager who looked well under eighteen, she had a small bulge he had thought, taking her for a child, was unshed baby fat—but now, he realized, could be the first showings of pregnancy.

Still, he could not have left her there for the days of the storm. Not once he had noticed her—noticed the sideways glances the sweaty man was giving her, impatient for Michael to leave. And so when, the SUV was finally ready, he turned to her politely, asked where she was going, and offered the pretty child a ride. Another mistake, he suspected. He appeared to be making a lot of them.

"How old are you?" he asked at last.

"Eighteen," she answered, mocking his solemn tone.

"Really?"

"Really, truly. As God is my witness. I turned eighteen just three weeks ago."

"And you are expecting?"

"Really, truly. As God is my witness. Just over two months now. Up the spout, as they say. Do they really say that? I've only heard it in movies. Anyways, two months gone. And that's why I want to get to Cheyenne. 'Cause that's where Corson is. He's the father, Corson, and his rock band is playing at a bar there. He's a dreamboat, and he's going to be famous someday, and is he ever going to be surprised to see me. The perfect Christmas present. I just decided all of a sudden. I texted him to say I was coming and took off for the airport."

While she looked down and smiled contentedly, Michael glanced at her, a tiny blonde girl with a pixie hairdo, an infectious smile too innocent for her, and an upturned nose. The signs of her pregnancy were apparent, once one knew. A glow to her skin that made her seem fresh and attractive. A lively healthiness, and peaking through her blouse, in the gaps between the strained buttons, the swell of her young breasts, enlarged, he supposed, by the pregnancy. Michael turned his eyes back to the road.

The first flurries were beginning, almost enough to turn on the windshield wipers.

"Did you ever read Dickens?" he asked.

"No. What's that? Is it any good?"

"Nothing. Just something about that man at the terminal reminded me of a Dickens character. I seem to be meeting them around every corner these days. But while I am thinking of it, why the private terminal?" he asked. "Why not a commercial flight? It is much more likely to get you where you are going."

"Oh, it's so neat." Cheyenne started almost bouncing in her seat. "Slider, the bass player in Corson's band, told me about it. He said that if you go where the private planes land in most cities, and you clean up and dress nice, like this skirt, and act friendly, sometimes somebody will let you hitch a ride. He said it didn't always click, but I've done it twice, and it ran like a dream for me, without hardly any wait at all. Once out to Los Angeles to see my friends from high school, and then back again to boring old Minneapolis. Both times, *bam!*, right on a plane, and all I had to do was make eyes at some nice old rich guy."

"And they did not pressure you to do anything more?" Michael asked carefully, an obscure anger rising in him like bile.

"Nah," she laughed. "Mostly they just wanted to talk, tell me how a little girl like me needs to be careful. And both times, they gave me some money. You understand how it is, a rich older guy like you."

Michael laughed. "Yes," he said, "I can see how that might work. But I am not rich, not the way truly rich people are rich. I am merely a work-a-day tax lawyer—one you would not glance at twice if you saw him on the street."

"Don't sell yourself short, Michael Going-to-Denver Stuyvesant. You've got that whole gray-hair gorgeous banker look going, with your oh-so-casual nice clothes and that stern, in-control moral thing that makes girls melt and think *oh-daddy-I-need-a-spanking*. I have lots of friends who would definitely do you. Besides, what do you mean, you're not rich? You have a private jet."

"No, I only borrowed it from someone who was not using it this week. There is a system for these things."

"Yeah," Cheyenne snorted. "A system for rich people. Anyways, if you're not rich, I could stand not being rich like you. Neat planes and neat cars like this one, and just anything you wanted. Free to go anywhere you wanted."

Michael reached down and turned the wipers up to full as the snow began to fall in earnest, marking the fields and the edges of the road with white and turning the black surface slick with moisture. As one drives in a storm, he thought, there is a field of flakes, out on the far edge of vision, where the snow seems to be falling normally, drifting down just as it does when one stares out a bedroom window. But closer in, there is a place where the flakes almost freeze, caught by the eye in stillness—and it is at that focal point that they seem to shift from falling down to sliding sideways directly toward the windshield. The danger, he knew, is the hypnosis: the eye mesmerized by that point into seeing nothing else, a false attentiveness half akin to sleep.

"Between the snowflakes," Cheyenne interrupted his reverie. "Wouldn't it be wonderful if we could drive between the snowflakes— going so fast, swerving so quick, that they never land on us? Like we were angels or something."

"What?" he asked, looking over as she stared out at the snow.

"Oh, I was just thinking," she said, turning again to smile at him. "I heard it on a TV show once. This guy says of the hero that 'he walks between the raindrops.' He didn't mean it in a nice way. He meant it as a warning to the hero's girlfriend—that everybody else gets hurt when the bullets fly, even if the hero always escapes. But I thought, like, wouldn't that be wonderful? To move like an angel between the raindrops, seeing them fall but never getting wet."

She laughed, a horsy sound. "Or passing through fire. I remember a preacher on the radio talking about the other gods in the Bible, and how they wanted children passed through fire. Like the raindrops or the snowflakes, but with flames. And that's what I want for my little guy," she said, patting her belly. "All safe through the warm and cold. Those other gods in the Bible. Jesus talks about them all the time, right?

"No."

"No?"

"No."

"What do you mean, 'no'?" she howled. "I mean, you can't just say *no* like a Ouija Board or something. You sound like my mom. No, no, no. All the time. No, no, no, no. That's not how, like, talking to people works. You have to *talk* to them, you know. That's why they call it *talking.*"

Michael Stuyvesant had never thought of himself as a seriously educated man. Not truly well read, not an intellectual—which meant, in the sense his grandfather would have used the word, someone whose primary focus in life is the high culture of art and the pursuit of philosophy and theology, all with a background of classical training in Greek and Latin. Even when the young lawyers in his white-shoe firm failed to catch a reference, he never felt an entirely unbridgeable gap between his old-fashioned education and theirs, however thin the modern curriculum of their prep schools and Ivy League colleges had grown.

But now with this girl, he could feel the gulf of ages. He stared out at the road, sighed, and began, "All right. The gospels describe two false gods in particular. The Old Testament names any number of other gods besides God the Father—including Moloch, who was not at all the kindly, St. Francis figure you seem to think him. 'Passed through fire' means"—he glanced over at her, saw again her youth—"um, not a nice thing. But the New Testament, the Christian story in the Bible, you understand?"

"Yes, I understand," Cheyenne answered with a petulant eye roll. "I'm not an idiot, you know. I went to church sometimes with my mom."

"Ah. Well, the New Testament speaks at length only about two of those false gods. Mammon and Caesar."

"Caesar wasn't a god. We read about him in school. He was just some general who got killed."

"The Romans declared several of the Caesars gods. By the time of Christ, the word just meant emperor, more or less, and the Jews, like all the other people in the empire, were supposed to at least pretend to worship him. In this context, *Caesar* means the state, the government. Power. And Mammon is a god of wealth. Jesus is speaking of the worship of money and the worship of power as the new false gods, replacing Moloch and the other old gods. Replacing even Yahweh, God the Father."

"That's you, isn't it? I mean, you're like a tax lawyer, sucking up to the government, and you're rich. I can see you with, like, a shrine and incense and stuff. Kneeling and praying, 'O, mighty Mammon. O great Caesar. I thank you for all my money and power, but give me more. Lots more. Amen.'"

He laughed. "No, a Mammon worshiper is someone more like you, my little friend. Listen to the way you talk about money. Listen to the way you talk about celebrities. The way the whole culture does."

"I don't want to worship money. I just want to have tons of it, so I can just have fun all the time. You know, the way it is on TV. Flying around, and throwing big parties, and meeting famous people, and buying lots of cool stuff, and getting your picture everywhere. Money sets you free."

"No."

"No?"

"No."

They laughed. Michael thought of saying that he did not have to worship money because he knew perfectly well what it was. Knew what it would buy and what it would not. He thought of telling the girl that money never set anyone free. It was just another possession, to be managed with all the rest and defined in a will when the time came for dying.

But how to explain to someone without any references or thought of experiences other than her own? Someone who was in mental essence a child, however grown-up her body? A child, as it happens, who suddenly screeched and pointed as he braked and swerved on the narrow highway that had seemed so empty, moments before, to avoid a car parked halfway into his lane—a jack lifting the car near the left rear tire and a red figure beside it waving the jack handle at them like a bludgeon as the big SUV slid by.

IV

By the time Michael had brought the Hummer back under control, straightened its skew across the road, and begun backing up, the red figure was leaning against his disabled car, beating the roof with the jack handle, puffs of snow flying up with each thwack.

"Why are you stopping, Michael?" Cheyenne moaned. "Don't stop. Keep going. We're going to get stuck in the snow, and he's some weirdo who'll probably steal your car and leave us here to freeze. C'mon, Michael. *Michael*, just go."

"Be quiet, please," he said, then twisted his face in a grin at the unlikeliness of Cheyenne's silence. He turned on the hazard lights, climbed down, and walked back toward the man, the ping of the Hummer's open-door warning like a small Christmas chime ringing out of time with the percussion clacks of the SUV's blinkers.

The man by the car was huge—more than huge: a giant with a long white beard—and he turned as Michael approached, the tire iron poised above his head. He looked, Michael thought, like a colossal figure about to take his turn on the High Striker machine at a carnival, the mallet ready to smash down on Michael's head and ring the bell. Or better maybe: Paul Bunyan poised to chop with his axe, if one could imagine Paul Bunyan dressed in the red velour jacket, baggy red pants, and black belt and boots of a super-sized shopping-mall Santa.

"Who the freaking hell are you?" the gargantuan shouted, weaving slightly like a tall pine about to topple. "Oh, whoops. Wash out my mouth. Mustn't curse in front of the kiddies. Who are you, kind sir, and what the hell do you want, you freaking busybody? Everywhere, freaking busybodies. Nosey-parker church ladies. You know what's wrong with this world? Nobody minds their own business. Nobody has the ordinary goddamn politeness to leave a man alone."

"Not to worry," Michael answered, spreading his hands in a calming gesture. "I only wondered if you could use a little help out here in the snow. A bad place to get a flat tire." The reek of whiskey seemed almost a physical presence, radiating from the man like heat from a fire.

"Oh, so you're my personal Santa, are you? A Santa sent to rescurate Santa. Um, I mean rescue. *Rescue* Santa. 'Cause that's what I am, you know: the best goddamn Santa in the world, whatever those church-lady prigs think down in Iowa. I'd like to take a whack at them. But"—he wove again, waggling the tire iron—"since you're here, you'll have to do, you freaking busybody. You nasty prying church lady."

Before the enormous red figure could stride forward, however, he lurched sideways against the snowy car and lowered his weapon. "Hmm," he said reflectively as though bemused by his new position, "except now that I think about it, maybe you're not Santa. Maybe you're my Rudolph. No, no, wait. I've got it. You're my own personal St. Bernard, sent through the snow from the monastery to save me. Where's the keg of brandy you're supposed to have around your neck, little doggy? Nice doggy. Good boy. 'Cause I do believe I could use another drink. Something better than the rotgut they sell down in Iowa. Sioux City, Iowa, my friend. It's hell on earth."

"No, I am sorry," Michael answered. "I do not have any liquor. But I believe there is some coffee in a thermos the service packed in the car. How about we put a little something warm in you, change your tire, and get you on your way before the storm locks everything down? That would be nice, yes?"

"Nice?" the Santa roared, straightening up to tower over Michael. "I freaking hate nice. And if you aren't my St. Bernard, well then, you're one of *them*, and your time on this earth is over, my busybody friend. I'll teach you to mind your own goddamn business." He raised the tire iron again. "I'll freaking teach you and all your kind, just"—his huge angry face turned suddenly gentle—"just as soon as I, ah, take a little nap here on the nice . . . soft . . . snow."

And with a surprising grace, the massive snow-flecked Santa Claus melted to his knees, paused for a moment, then tumbled slowly onto his face—the tire iron still held above him until it fell from his opening fingers to tap him on the back of the head while Michael stumbled vainly forward to catch it.

"*Michael! Michael, oh my God, Michael! What did you do?*" he heard in a shriek behind him as he picked up the fallen weapon. He turned to see Cheyenne's head poking sideways out the open driver's-side door. Her elfin face, he thought distractedly—the triangular, foxlike face of an elf who thought he had just killed Santa Claus. And what else would she think? Michael Stuyvesant, a man who prided himself on the calm order of his life, stood with a tire iron in his hand, straddling the body of a titanic Kris Kringle while the fat snowflakes drifted down around him and the chiming, clicking noises of an expensive SUV merged with the screams of a pregnant teenager.

"Oh, shut up," he said.

V

The moral effort necessary to force any kind of competence out of Cheyenne surprised Michael—exhausted him, in fact, almost as much as the physical effort of dealing with the drunken Santa Claus in his weakened condition.

Ann. God, how he missed Ann. She would have been at her best in a situation like this: calm, strong, useful, a companion for an emergency. A friend for the road. "Were you brought up by wolves?" he finally snapped when Cheyenne whined for a third time that they should just leave the man in the snow and drive on, quick before someone saw them and called the police.

Maybe it was his open disgust that eventually persuaded Cheyenne to agree to drive the SUV. She was certainly no use with the rest, refusing to help as he manhandled the body into the back seat of the disabled car, wriggling the huge man inside, inch by inch, for what seemed like an hour. But eventually, Santa safe from frostbite, Michael finished changing the tire and climbed, white as a snowman, behind the wheel of the man's old Chevrolet to lead the way back toward civilization.

A series of cell-phone calls with his efficient secretary back east had confirmed what the lack of traffic on the two-lane feeder highway suggested: He had lost too much time. The interstate he had meant to drop down to take—I-90 to Sioux Falls and beyond—was closing, the secretary confirmed with the state police, and he would have been turned back before he even got out of Minnesota. The nearest place with any kind of medical help was the town of Sleepy Eye, fifteen miles behind him. The county clinic had closed a few years earlier, but the local nurse practitioner had been retained by his secretary. The nurse would meet him downtown at the Northern Lights, the only hotel in the area to answer the phone, where the seldom-used Governor's Suite and a pair of single rooms on either side of it had been reserved for him and his, ahem, *guests*, as his secretary so delicately described the menagerie he seemed to be collecting—a train of holiday oddities, like the streams of animals some people put out with their Christmas crèches.

And, par for the course of this trip, he thought, Sleepy Eye's cafés and even its bars were closed, forcing Michael to head to the local convenience store for food after he had gotten everyone checked into the hotel. He had not actually been inside one of those stores, he realized, since they all added credit-card readers to their gas pumps—and even before that, he thought of them as existing solely for the people buying beer, cigarettes, and lottery tickets as they waited impatiently in line to pay for a tank of gas. Still, *someone* must shop at such places, or why would they bother stocking shelves with pre-packaged food and toiletries?

In fact, as he walked the aisles of the Gas 'n' Guzzle, Michael Stuyvesant could not remember the last time he had done any food shopping. It was not that he thought himself above such things. He simply did not need to shop for himself, and at least since Ann had died, he had felt little interest in visiting the butcher or baker, much less a supermarket.

Santa Claus—Nils Johanssen from Finnmark, North Dakota, the man's driver's license claimed—was in no condition to eat, according to the annoyed nurse in the heavy parka who had met them at the hotel. Anxious to get back to her house before the snow stranded her and ruined her lutefisk Christmas-season dinner, she had helped roll the giant into a bed, cleaned and bandaged his head, and given him a B-12 vitamin injection and some fluids. Explaining with a sniff that he would wake in the morning with the terrible hangover he no doubt deserved, she had covered the snoring man with a blanket, set precisely two painkiller pills on the nightstand for the morning, and left—plotting to mail Michael's

secretary a bill that would, by rural Minnesota standards, make that un-pleasantly efficient person from the East Coast think twice about sending out the county's best registered nurse practitioner for a case of public drunkenness.

Still, even with the Santa-suited Nils Johannsen taken care of, Michael had to find something at the convenience store from which to make a meal for himself and Cheyenne, who had stumbled in, her clothes sopping wet from the snow, and promptly fallen asleep on the Governor's Suite's large bed. He wandered in wonder among the convenience-store shelves, look-ing at the breakfast cereals and instant mixes and strange cans of forgotten vegetables.

The chips alone were half an aisle: Lays and Ruffles and Pringles. Beer chips and kettle-cooked vinegar chips in faux paper bags, designed to look like some fantasy of old-fashioned packaging. Fritos and Doritos and Tosti-dos—triangles dusted in carcinogenic orange: waste from a movie-set's nu-clear-power plant certain to melt down by the movie's end.

And following them were the shelves of Kraft Easy Mac Cup and Kraft Jet Puffed Marshmallows and Kraft Macaroni and Cheese, different some-how from the Kraft Easy Mac Cup. Kraft Original Barbecue Sauce and Kraft Parmesan Cheese. Kraft Ranch Dressing, Kraft Squeeze Mayonnaise, and Kraft Squeeze Miracle Whip, which was not mayonnaise in some un-known but apparently essential way.

And then all the coffees that, he realized, he had assumed the gentrify-ing of American hot drinks over the previous twenty years had banished into the forgotten darkness of lost brands. Folgers. Yuban and Butternut. Chock Full o' Nuts and Hills Brothers. Maxwell House Original. All the thin brown stuff, barely darker than tea, that diners used to keep simmering in a percolator for hours at time. And then Nescafé, Sanka, Taster's Choice—the brands of instant hot drinks that almost brought coffee-drink-ing to end in America during the 1970s and 1980s. The spouses of junior partners, he remembered, used to serve the stuff at dinner parties as though it were a great, hip improvement, the undissolved fragments melting on the side of the cup in oily droplets.

His sense of the strangeness of it all was, he suspected, an effect of his tiredness and the long day. Or perhaps it came from the alternating chill of the snow and warmth of the car, aggravated by the medication he had taken, true to his doctor's schedule, at the hotel. For that matter, his fascination with the convenience store probably owed something to the focusing of the mortally ill, that ironic gift of pre-announced death—for somewhere, not all that deep in his mind, he knew he would never have this experience again. Never see, never touch, this part of life again.

But whatever the cause, he roamed the Gas 'n' Guzzle convenience store in Sleepy Eye, Minnesota, with an amazement he could not recall since his mad cigar-smoking older cousin had taken him to New York as a child to visit the FAO Schwarz toy store. Like that child again, almost, he walked the aisles with little of the middle ground of normal experience. A sharp, nearly painful focus on the sheer particularity of each object: its weight in his hand, its plastic smell, its crinkly sound, the variations in color. And yet, at the same time, a great abstraction, as though he floated above his body, unconcerned with himself, or the need to choose something, or even the increasingly suspicious eye the clerk was turning on him. Outside, beyond the Christmas images—reindeer, candy canes, triangular pine trees—soaped on the Gas 'n' Guzzle's windows, he could see the falling snow, still piling up, silent and clean.

The vibrations of his cell phone called Michael back to something resembling normalcy, and on the other end he found a panicked Cheyenne, asking where he was.

"Did you not see my note?" he asked.

"Well, yeah, kind of," she answered. "That's where I found this phone number. But I . . . ah, couldn't read the rest of it."

"Why not?"

"It's really nice. I mean, you have beautiful handwriting, and I wanted to put it away somewhere safe and save it for ever and ever, but I . . . oh, I'm sorry, but I can't read cursive very well. I thought you'd left me here at the hotel and were saying goodbye or something. But I could read the number, and I thought, well, no he wouldn't leave his cell-phone number, if that's what he was doing. But then I thought, well, maybe he would, if, like, he was that kind of responsible guy and wanted to make sure I was safe, even after he beat up Santa Claus. Which I understand, believe me. I mean, the guy totally deserved it, threatening us like that, and I've decided to tell the police that's why you were so brave and punched his lights out, if you especially want me to, although my mom always told me never to talk to the police, since what they really want is something to blame you for, even if you were just a witness. Anyways, once I knew that I would be brave too, and testify for you if you needed it, I couldn't think why you would leave me. So I decided to call. Are you leaving me? Here in Sleepy Eye? I guess I could get back to Minneapolis by myself, hitch a ride or something, but it would make me sad."

"No, Cheyenne," Michael laughed. "I am not leaving you to fend for yourself. Not just yet, anyway. As I said in my note, I have only gone out to find us some food. I will be back in a few minutes. Meanwhile, the room next to mine is for you. You should get yourself cleaned up and warm. The food selection is not great, I am afraid, but I will bring what I can find here at the convenience store. Is there anything in particular you want?"

"Ooh, wafer cookies," she squealed. "Just last night I was dreaming of wafer cookies. Vanilla, with that raised crisscross pattern on them. Aren't girls like me supposed to want pickles and ice cream? It's what they do in movies, but maybe that comes later. Right now, all I want is wafer cookies. And something good to drink. Thank you, Michael Not-Going-to-Denver-Yet Stuyvesant. I'll be waiting."

When he got back to his hotel room, the huge black SUV having powered like a tank through the still-falling snow, Michael found Cheyenne sitting cross-legged on his bed, looking at her cell phone.

"I just texted Corson to say that I wasn't going to make it to Wyoming tonight, after all. Still no answer from him. He gets like that when he and the band are practicing really hard. But, oh, what did you buy? I'm starving. Famished. Isn't that one of your kind of words? *Famished.* But you don't have a British accent, so maybe not. Anyways, I could eat a horse. A horse made of wafer cookies. Couldn't you?"

Michael set the bags from the store down on a table and began to unpack them. "We are eating off paper napkins, I am afraid. There do not seem to be any plates. But if you could bring over those glasses I see on the counter, I will set up a snack for us here."

In the end, it was the refrigerated section of the store he had raided, choosing the best-looking package of a local cheddar, a tube of summer sausage, and some apples. Plus a small pocketknife he had purchased to slice them with. A box of saltine crackers and a package of wafer cookies. A bottle of beer and a quart of milk.

"What we will do for breakfast, I am not sure, but this at least should see us through the night."

"I like wine better," Cheyenne said, coming to join him. "Don't you? But here in stupid Minnesota they don't sell it in the little supermarkets and convenience stores. Only beer. But that's okay. Corson likes beer, so I guess I should get used to it."

The stillness of the older man's hands caught her attention. "Oh, you think I'm too young for beer, don't you?"

"I, ah, . . . " Michael began.

"Oh, no, I know. You think it's bad for the little guy," Cheyenne interrupted, patting her belly. "I heard where they don't say that anymore about alcohol. At least not for small amounts. But maybe you're right. I like how you're always taking care of people, like getting the nurse for Santa. That's why you bought the milk for me, isn't it? Well, I can drink milk."

Even the milk and crackers with cheese, sausage, and apple slices were not enough to keep her quiet long.

"My older brother used to do this," Cheyenne explained, putting a whole cracker in her mouth with only the corners sticking out—then biting down so the corners pointed up toward her cheeks to form pointy teeth. "Grr, grr," she growled before dissolving in laughter, the cracker corners falling into her lap. "Just like a bulldog. Oh, I was kind of scared, when he would do it, me in my high chair and him growling like an angry bulldog. But then he'd laugh, and I would beg him to do it again and again and again."

She brushed the crumbs onto the floor. "I wish I was a child again, don't you? Things were less important then. Or maybe I mean more important, like the crackers and the bulldog. The little stuff mattered more, and the big stuff didn't matter at all. I mean, it's like, I didn't ever really know my father. He moved away to Houston or someplace. But that was okay, because my older brother Timothy was there, and he used to tell me stories. Great stories about my stuffed animals going for walks and having adventures, and then coming home safe and drinking a glass of milk. Do you like stories? You must know thousands. Tell me a story."

The mention of a brother was new and set Michael's mind to working. "Where is he, your brother? Do you stay in touch?"

Cheyenne looked away. "He's gone. Timothy had a big fight with my mom, when I was twelve, and he joined the army. He was killed in an accident at his army base a few months later. We had a funeral and everything, but I miss him. Anyways," she smiled, turning back to catch him with her pixie eyes, "tell me the story you promised."

"I never promised a story."

"As good as. You didn't say no." Cheyenne curled up on the bed with a pair of wafer cookies and pulled up the coverlet, still rumpled from her earlier nap. "C'mon. Something good. I'm not sleepy at all."

And so Michael Stuyvesant laughed, and while he cleaned up from their impromptu dinner, he told the girl who called herself Cheyenne the first story that popped into his mind—the tale of Eldorado Johnny, Langford Peel, and the Washoe gold mines of western Nevada.

"So," he began, "back in the days of the gold rush . . . "

"One upon a time," Cheyenne interrupted.

"What?"

"Stories, real stories, are supposed to begin 'Once upon a time,' but when I was little I couldn't pronounce it right, so Timothy always started his stories the way I said it: 'One upon a time.'"

"Ah," Michael sighed. "All right. One upon a time, back in the days of the Wild West, there was a gold-rush town in the Nevada mountains called Virginia City.

"And the chief of the town was a man named Langford Peel—the chief, meaning the sheriff or the peacekeeper, more or less. The hard man, the gunfighter, who probably was not the most moral character himself but who at least made sure that the miners did not get completely out of hand. The man who insisted that some small basis of society continued to exist. Do you know what I mean? Women and children not openly assaulted on the street, people not robbed on their way to church on a Sunday morning, the bodies of the dead treated respectfully. Virginia City was a wild place in a wild time, but some of the root stuff of civilization existed there because a few men like Peel demanded it and were strong enough to make it so."

He carried their glasses over to the bar sink and rinsed them out, carefully and precisely, then set them upside down on the edge of the sink to dry. "'Farmer' Peel, they called him, although I'm not sure why. An educated man, a Harvard student, they say, who had come West to escape what he thought were the over-civilized rules of East Coast life. It is an irony, I suppose, that a man fleeing civilization in the East would find himself building civilization in the West. But, then, he did have to kill six men in gunfights in the early days of the gold camp, so perhaps he found what he was looking for."

A nausea suddenly took him, souring his stomach and making him lean over the sink, supporting himself against the counter. The doctors had warned that these bouts of weakness would happen more and more often as the end came.

"Are you all right?" Cheyenne asked, sitting up on the bed.

Michael waved her off. "I am fine. Just a little indigestion. Something that did not sit right."

He straightened up and began closing the packages of cheese and meat. "Where was I? Oh, yes, Virginia City. So the town grew, and the reputation of Farmer Peel spread—till it came to the ears of Eldorado Johnny over in the Colorado River country. Johnny was a boy, a young man, maybe seventeen or eighteen, about your age. And one day he decided he had heard enough, heard too much, in fact, of this talk about the great Langford Peel. If Peel was a fake, then Johnny was going to expose him. And if Peel really was a great man, well then, that was all right, too. Johnny was born to be great himself, he knew, and the time of his greatness was upon him. So he strapped on his gun and made his way west to Virginia City."

"Oh," said Cheyenne. "This is fantastic. Like a movie or a poem or something. So what happened next?"

"Eldorado Johnny met Farmer Peel, of course. But he stopped first to get his hair cut, all neat, and to have his boots polished so bright he could see his reflection in them. He put on his best clothes, a red scarf around his neck, and he glittered when he walked. Down the main street of Virginia City he came, looking for its chief, only to find him in Lynch's Saloon, drinking in the early afternoon. 'I have come to shoot you down, Langford Peel,' he announced to the barroom. 'By this time tomorrow, I aim to be either chief of Virginia City or the best-looking corpse in the graveyard.'"

Michael wet a washcloth from the bathroom and began wiping the table at which they had eaten. "Peel tried to talk him out of it, of course—said he would rather drink with the boy than shoot him. But Johnny would not be dissuaded. So out they walked into the bright sun of the street, the young man from the ranch even more polite than his Harvard-educated opponent, each giving way to the other."

He rinsed the washcloth, wrung it out, and spread it to dry on the curved neck of the bar sink's spout. "But once they were outside, Johnny knew better than to hesitate. He twirled, flashing into the fancy move he had been practicing for weeks. And that hard man Langford Peel waited a heartbeat, just so everyone could see that Johnny had gone for his pistol first. And then he shot him. Put the young man down like a dog. Three bullets, one to the throat, one to the chest, one to the head, before Eldorado Johnny could get off more than a single wild, misaimed shot."

Michael at last sat down, in a chair across the room from the girl. "And that was that. Peel paid for the funeral, and the whole town got drunk on the strength of it. He always said that he regretted shooting the boy, but I am doubtful. He must have known how the story would add to his reputation. Still, Langford Peel also said that he was the only person there who really understood Eldorado Johnny, and that I do believe. The young man had been honorable, according to his lights, and honor . . . honor is not nothing. For a man like Peel, at least."

Cheyenne tilted her head and gave Michael Stuyvesant a speculative look. He had forgotten she was not stupid, exactly. Just silly and uneducated, unserious—drifting on the ephemeral power of a girl's first attractiveness. "I was sure you would give me a Christmas story," she said at last. "And it really wasn't one, was it?"

"No," he answered. "Not exactly."

"Still," she nodded. "I think I see maybe . . . oh, oh," she squealed as her cell phone began to chime the opening to Jingle Bells. "It's Corson. Finally. I"—jumping up and heading toward the bathroom—"I'm sorry, Michael, but I have to talk to him. I'll be right back."

He wriggled and rearranged himself on the lumpy wing-backed chair. Had he really grown so spoiled that he could not stand the mild discomfort of bad hotel furniture, or had the cancer and its treatment simply stripped him of the normal reserves of flexibility and endurance that allow the body to ignore minor distress? He could hear water running in the bathroom, Cheyenne naively covering her voice he imagined, and he smiled.

Michael was checking the weather on his cell phone—there was a possibility, he saw, that at least the main roads would be open to four-wheel-drive vehicles like his SUV the next morning—when he heard the water turn off and the door to the bathroom open. It was not till several minutes had passed, however, that Michael realized Cheyenne had not come out, and with a groan at his stiffness, he unfolded himself from the chair and went to look for her.

He found her sitting on the edge of the bathtub, holding her cell phone against her chest and sobbing. She was not a good crier. His wife Ann, he remembered, seemed to grow more beautiful when she cried—tearing up at the implausibly happy endings of sentimental movies or the pathetic scenes in Dickens's stories when she read them aloud to him on long drives. Even Jane Austen could make her cry, at the right moment, and she would squeeze his arm, her eyes wet and glowing with the happy sadness of nostalgia on hearing again any of half a dozen minor pop songs that were on the radio when they first met. Cheyenne cried instead like a child: racked with sobs, her face a blotchy red, and the mucus bubbling at her nose. Michael Stuyvesant sat beside the girl on the uncomfortable bathtub edge, put his arm around her, and pulled her sideways against him.

"He said . . . he said he didn't want me," she moaned. "Corson said the baby wasn't his, and he didn't know me, and I would just have to take care of it."

She broke down again, wetting his shirt for minutes before she could continue. And even then, Michael barely listened to the details—a litany of cruelty he realized he had half expected: The would-be rock star was leaving Wyoming, destination undisclosed, and would not take responsibility for anything. If she kept bothering him, he would have friends hunt her down and beat her. If she needed cash for an abortion she could just turn more tricks on the street, since the only girl he remembered sleeping with in Minneapolis was some blonde prostitute too stupid to take the money off the dresser when he was done with her.

Through it all, Michael held her, saying over and over, "Shhh, shhh. It will be all right. Everything will be all right." And when she was calm enough, he rose, took the cell phone from her, and set it beside the sink. Dampening a towel, he knelt in front of her on the tile floor and cleaned her face with a gentle firmness. Then he raised her up and carried her into the other room, settling her on his bed, whispering still, "Shhh. It will be all right. Everything will be all right."

He had intended only to set her down and cover her, but she held him too strongly, pulling him down beside her. Michael reached out for the coverlet and pulled it over them as well as he could while Cheyenne clung to him, and the pair lay unmoving, just the older man holding the girl on the hotel bed.

I have gotten too old for this, Michael thought when after half hour his arm had fallen asleep and the pins and needles in it grew too much to bear. He tried to disengage gently, but the motion was enough to rouse the girl.

"Thank you, Michael," she said, hugging him tight for a moment before allowing him to sit up against the headboard and massage his arm. Cheyenne stared up at him for a moment, then pushed back the cover and rose clumsily to her knees, sitting on her heels.

"I'm a mess," she announced, as though it were a surprise, when she caught a look of herself in the mirror above the dresser. She made an awkward attempt to comb her hair with her fingers, straighten her blouse, and smooth her skirt, before staring down at her hands in her lap for a long moment.

"You've been so good to me," Cheyenne said quietly. "To me, to Santa, to everybody." Meeting his eyes through her bangs, she reached out and put her hands on his chest. "So good, Michael Not-Going-to-Denver-Tonight Stuyvesant," she whispered and kissed him, melting against his chest.

The middle ground is morality, Michael realized in a strange abstraction. On one side is disconnected thought, a floating above the self while he wondered—calmly and unhurriedly, as though he had all the time in the world to figure it out—how he had arrived at this. And on the other side was the sharp particularity of her soft lips, her fresh skin, the weight of her young, full breasts against him. He could not remember the last time he wanted a woman as much as he wanted this girl. She felt so alive in his arms. She felt like life itself.

But she was not, he knew, and when Cheyenne raised herself off him to begin unbuttoning his shirt, he caught her hands gently and stopped her.

"No," he said.

"No?" she smiled at him

"No. Not me, not now."

"Are you sure?" she asked, taking his hand in hers and kissing his palm. "I'll make you feel wonderful, the way you make me feel. I'll take care of you, just like you take care of me. I'm not your daughter, you know."

"No," Michael answered. He freed his hand and pulled her down against his chest. "And you are not my wife," he said. "You are just a confused girl going through a rough time, and you think you need someone to want you."

"I can hear your heart beating," Cheyenne answered.

"Shhh. Just sleep," he murmured. "We'll talk tomorrow."

But when Michael Stuyvesant awoke the next morning, the room was empty. Cheyenne had packed her things and gone.

VI

"I saw your girlfriend this morning," said Santa as Michael came into his room to check on him.

"Cheyenne?"

"Yep. The cute little blonde piece with the belly. You do like 'em young, don't you, you sly dog? I might have helped her out myself, if my freaking head didn't hurt like hell."

The enormous man winced, sitting at the table in an undershirt and his Santa pants, and took a careful sip of water from the glass dwarfed in his hand. "Speaking of which," he began in embarrassment. "About yesterday . . ."

"What did she say? I mean, I am sorry to have interrupted you," Michael interrupted. "But before we get to that, I need to know if she said anything. She is not my girlfriend, only someone I picked up on my travels yesterday. But she has disappeared this morning, and I do want to be certain she is all right."

"Kind of what I figured," Nils answered. "You were gathering strays yesterday, weren't you? But she had the look that told me something else was up."

"What look?"

"Oh, you know. Or maybe you don't. A rich guy like you probably doesn't ever get desperate, the way the rest of us do. Anyway, not the look of a liar exactly, somebody who lies all the time just for the hell of it. But the look that says you can't trust anything this person is about to say because they're desperate and will say anything. A cornered-rat look. It's all in the eyes and the way they hold their hands. Get around a little more, outside your rich folks' life, and you'll see what I mean. 'The mass of men lead lives of quiet desperation.' Henry David Thoreau said that, and who would know better? I read *Walden* again every spring, just for the comedy. What? You didn't think a department-store Santa would read Thoreau?"

"I had not stopped to think about it," Michael answered, "but of course you would, if you were a reader. Cheyenne, though. What did she say?"

"Oh, some cock-and-bull story about how you were her lover, and you had knocked her up, and now you were driving her up and down the State of Minnesota, pressuring her to do something she didn't want. It wasn't clear what, exactly—but whoo, boy, did she make you sound like hot stuff. So much wild sex, she said, that she couldn't think straight, and she needed to get away from you to decide what to do. She asked me to drive her back to her mother's house in Minneapolis."

The white-bearded giant took another cautious sip. "As I say, I might have done it, even though I knew she was lying. I was supposed to drive to Port de Grâce, clear up by the Canadian border, but it looks like I'm going to miss the gig, so I would have had time to swing by Minneapolis. The girl seemed just a little young for me, truth be told. But hell, if the daughter looks like that, maybe the momma is worth a visit. Still, I hurt too much, so I told her no."

Nils cleared his throat and put his hands on the table as though to brace himself for a blow. "And speaking of hurting, about yesterday, I may have been a trifle under the weather. I won't say I genuinely needed your help, but, hell, I'm man enough to thank you for it, and I must apologize if I said anything unseemly to you or your young companion. I would have sworn there wasn't any way that someone like you could have KO'd me, put me down for the count, no matter how . . . ill I was feeling. But there it is, a fact's a fact, and as I said, I'm man enough to admit it. If you'd shake my hand, I'd be honored. There's more to you than meets the eye, my friend, as our little Cheyenne was saying just this morning."

It took another hour to finish up with Santa. A kind of old-fashioned etiquette seemed to guide the men, as though they were the last two people left who understood the dance. While they shared a pot of coffee ordered up from room service, Michael began by refusing repayment for Nils's hotel room. Then, of course, he allowed himself to be persuaded to accept it, just as soon as Nils should have the money to give him. At last, assuring the man that his car was in the parking lot, the keys over the visor, and giving him his card, Michael shook the giant's hand again and said goodbye.

He felt a curious reluctance to leave. Some flights seemed to be getting out. And since Sleepy Eye was almost exactly half way between Sioux Falls and Minneapolis, and the western airports were clearing faster, Michael had his secretary make arrangements to have him return the rented SUV in South Dakota and take a commercial flight, Sioux Falls to Denver, late that evening. Which gave him little to do for the next few hours except putter around his hotel room and then make the slow drive west. He could use the lack of agitation, he decided. The previous day had taken more out of him than he had expected at this stage of his illness.

He was just thinking about a nap, before the drive, when his phone buzzed, vibrating on the countertop.

Pressing the speaker button to answer the call, he heard a tinny voice saying, "Michael. Michael, is that you?"

"Cheyenne?"

"Oh, Michael, I'm sorry I ran away without saying goodbye. It's just that you didn't want me, and you were going on to Denver, so I tried to leave quietly. But Michael, they hurt me. I'm sorry, but I didn't know who else to call. They hurt me, and I think they hurt the baby, and I'm scared they'll come back. Please, can you help me, one more time?"

"Where are you, Cheyenne? Do you want me to call the police? An ambulance?"

"No, Michael, please, only you. I think the men are coming back, but you can fight them, just like you did Santa. I was trying to get back to Minneapolis, and these men said they would give me a ride. But then they wanted me to do things, and I said no, just like you did. So they hit me, but I fought them off, and jumped out of the car, and ran through the snow and hid. I'm in a barn, only like twenty miles east on the highway. It's bright red, right after a blue farmhouse. Oh, Michael, please come."

Michael was already out of the hotel and climbing into his SUV by the time he told her to keep hidden, hold onto her phone, and wait for him.

He found Cheyenne a half an hour later, tucked behind a trough in a cow barn, while the owner, a round-bellied dairy farmer named Sigurd Boe, tried to lure her out, talking to her as gently and strangely as would to a wild animal.

"She's scaring my cows," he explained to Michael. "They don't like excitement. They don't like crazy city girls. They don't like anything except peace. I saw her running across the pasture and into the barn. A couple of men in a car were coming up the driveway after her, but when they saw me they backed out and drove off. So maybe I understand why she thought she had to hide. But she has to go now. My cows don't like it. Too much excitement in this weather makes their milk sour, and I don't like it when my cows give sour milk. I could call the pastor's wife, maybe, if you need help rooting her out."

Michael Stuyvesant was wondering himself just how much assistance he would need to bring her out without frightening her more or getting himself trampled. But then he heard a moo, a rustle among the cattle, and Cheyenne's voice calling out, "Michael? Michael, is that you? Oh, thank God, you came."

VII

It was his secretary naturally, who like some distant angel took care of the details. By the time Michael had packed the injured girl in his SUV and reached the outskirts of Minneapolis, a hundred miles east of Sigurd Boe's barn, his flight had been rescheduled for early the next morning out of the Minneapolis/St. Paul airport, a hotel had been booked for him, and a private room had been found for the girl at St. Mary Magdalene's University Hospital.

Cheyenne, the suspicious doctors would eventually tell him—once they were convinced that Michael was the girl's rescuer, not her attacker—had bruising on her cheek but no concussion, they thought, as a result of the blow to the head. The scratches and bruises on her arms and legs were relatively minor, whether the result of her first struggles, her rolling out of the moving car, or her running across the snowy field and climbing in among the cows.

About the blow to her abdomen, however, they were less sanguine. She had been punched in the side with some considerable force, and she was passing blood. The fetus, they suggested, may not have been harmed, but she was, when all was said and done, a very small person with little extra protection for an unborn child. She did not appear to have made any prior visits to an obstetrician or even to have had a regular relation with a gynecologist, and after her attack she would need regular monitoring during the entire course of her pregnancy.

Michael thanked them gravely and politely, left his secretary's phone number with the billing coordinator, bought a teddy bear at the gift shop, and rode the elevator up to Cheyenne's floor, listening to the complicated and flirtatious tale of a wild weekend a pair of young doctors were trying to tell a nurse.

He found the girl on her side in her hospital bed, staring at a large bouquet in a deep green vase—red roses, pinecones, pine needles, and some lily-like white blossoms he did not recognize: the Christmas-themed flowers he should have known his secretary would arrange for the room.

"Hello, Michael Still-Not-in-Denver Stuyvesant," Cheyenne said, not taking her eyes off the flowers. "I'm glad you came."

"I brought you this," he said, setting the teddy bear on the bed beside her. "For you and the baby, eventually. The doctors tell me you are going to be fine, if you just rest up and follow their recommendations."

"I know," she answered quietly, reaching out and pulling the bear into a cuddle against her chest.

"I have to leave soon, if I am going to reach Denver to see my family in time for Christmas."

"I know that, too."

"You should call your mother. You are eighteen and expecting, so they will treat you as adult, but the hospital would be much happier if there were a responsible relative they could call."

"I will," she answered dully. "Tomorrow."

"There are people here who will talk with you, if you want. A woman's counselor, a psychologist, a priest. They will call the police for you, if you're ready, to take down a description of the men who attacked you."

"Not now. Maybe tomorrow."

Michael sat with her quietly for the next few hours, her silence broken only by her request, whenever he rose to stretch, that he not leave quite yet. Eventually, though, when her eyes closed and breathing fell, he decided that he would go and let her sleep. He was almost out the door when he heard her call out sharply.

"Are you all right, Cheyenne? Is anything wrong?" he turned back to ask, finding her half-raised up in bed and staring at him anxiously.

"No. It's all right. I just . . . I just wondered if maybe you could tell me one more story before you had to go."

"I am out of stories," he answered. "It has been an exhausting day or two, and I am not sure how much longer I can last."

"Just one, just a little one. Please."

Michael Stuyvesant sat down in the chair facing her, his overcoat on his lap. "All right," he said. "One story. But only if you smile."

"What?"

"Only if you sit up like a big girl"—he plumped the pillows behind her back, helping her up—"and smile for me that goofy smile like the Cheyenne who has been spending hours and hours with me. The real Cheyenne, the one I remember. The one who could not stop talking if her life depended on it. The one who was sure she could charm an old man into driving her halfway across the country."

She giggled, put her hand to her mouth as though to stop, then slowly took it away and smiled at him. "Oh, Michael. We had such fun, didn't we? I didn't even mind that, no matter what we did, we weren't getting any closer to Wyoming. Do you remember when you punched out the giant Santa with the tire iron? I looked out just in time to see him go down, blam, like a huge tree falling. I was still scared, but you—you were a hero.

I think I knew all along Corson was going to be a bastard. A nasty creep who didn't want me. I just kept going because it was an adventure. A crazy, wonderful time, and I liked being with you."

"There my girl is. Now just keep being yourself, and let me think of a good story."

She arranged the teddy bear on her lap to listen. "My brother Timothy used to tell me stories, did I tell you that? About teddy bears, all my stuffed animals, who would go out for walks and have adventures. I think I'll call this one Michael."

"That is nice of you, and yes, I remember about your brother. Now be quiet and listen. One upon a time," he began, and Cheyenne giggled again.

"Yes," he intoned in his storyteller's voice, "one upon a time, there was a man named Odysseus. Ulysses, the Romans would call him: a good name. For a long while, Ulysses had been forced to be away from his family, fighting the Trojans with the rest of his Greek friends. But at last, after many years, he was finally free to sail back home to the wonderful island of Ithaca and his beautiful wife and son. He was a clever man, the cleverest in all of Greece—the one who had thought up the trick of the Trojan Horse, winning the war—and he supposed that the gods loved him. But even clever men need to learn hard lessons about the gods."

Michael studied the girl for a moment. "He sailed for home, but the sea was unforgiving, and he seemed to make no progress. Adventure after adventure, he and his men had. But always, at the key moment, they were blown off course or shipwrecked or forced to sail out of their way. Ulysses spent as many years at sea, trying to get home, as he had spent away at the war, and he often doubted that the god of the sea would ever allow him passage."

Cheyenne made the teddy bear wipe a tear from its eye and gesture with a paw for him to continue. "Yes, well, I could tell you about all those adventures, and how eventually Ulysses managed miraculously to arrive in Ithaca, reclaiming his house and joining with his now-grown son to drive out all the men who had been pestering his wife. But I want to tell you instead about what he did after all that—what he did once his home was settled and his family safe."

He looked down at his overcoat, brushing it gently as though it still had snow on it. "Even with everything well, and roses and smiles all around, Ulysses knew that he had not yet arrived at the ending of his story, however close it seemed. So he took an oar, one of those long things that he and his men had used through all their years at sea, and he put it over his shoulder. And then he began to walk inland, mile after mile, further and further from the sea. He walked for days, weeks, until at last he met a man who asked why he was carrying a grain paddle—a man who lived so far from the coast that he did not know what an ocean-going oar was. And do you know what Ulysses did then?"

Cheyenne shook her head solemnly.

"He built a temple to the god of the sea, there where no one knew that god, as payment for his safe return across the water from Troy to Ithaca."

"A big temple?" she asked. "Marble, gold, all that stuff?"

"No," Michael answered, rising from his chair and putting on his overcoat. "Just a clean, solid little place. Nothing more, nothing less. Dry-set stone walls and a roof, a small altar. The kind of thing a man good with hands could build by himself, if kept at it for a few weeks, working steadily during the daylight hours and camping out at night beneath the stars. And when he was done, he carved a dedication to the god of the sea, knelt and said his prayers, and walked the long way back home."

"I thought at least this one would be a Christmas story, Michael Finally-Going-to-Denver Stuyvesant."

"So did I. So did I." He leaned over and kissed her on the forehead. "Be well, Cheyenne. Be well."

On his way out of St. Mary Magdalene's, Michael noticed the hospital chapel, all dressed up in its penitential Advent purple, and he stopped with some ironic self-consciousness to light a candle for the girl. His family had always been Episcopalians, but Ann was a Catholic, something of a to-do in the family at the time of their marriage, and she would have approved. On the flight to Denver, he remembered her, heavy with their second child, explaining to him that all pregnant women are beautiful, because they are signs, visible reflections, of the Blessed Virgin Mary—in all her future joy and all her future pain and sorrow. And every baby, she added defiantly while he laughed and tickled her, is a sign of Christ, so full of promise and infinite possibility. Ann had been such a sentimentalist, too much sometimes, but he had to admit that Cheyenne had seemed beautiful to him in some new, personal way he could not quite categorize: neither wife nor daughter nor lover.

In Denver, his son and daughter and their families were glad to see him, however unexpectedly. They were disturbed, naturally, by the news about his cancer and gravely concerned about his care in the coming months. They were, in fact, all that he hoped and expected they would be—all that he and the old blueblood system of American wealth had formed them to be: polite and kind, deeply caring in their practical and efficient way. They allowed him to speak quietly, at his own pace, about lawyers, the disposal of trust funds, the big family house back east, the summer place in upstate New York. The necessary arrangements, the required settlements. They spoke, too, about Ann, reaching out to touch his hand softly while they did so.

Michael Stuyvesant died in his home early that spring, "after a long illness bravely borne," as the newspaper obituary said—a line his son had insisted be inserted, knowing his father would have smiled a little sardonically at its old-fashioned correctness.

A few eyebrows were raised, when the will was read, by the large but not, in the end, overly extravagant bequest for his secretary—together with Michael's instructions to pay the obstetrical bills of a very young woman in Minnesota and to establish a college fund for her yet-to-born child. A hint of scandal, perhaps, but since their father's most confidential lawyer assured them that the estate would never be sued for child support or a share of their inheritance, Michael's children decided it was some secret fling of their father's, and they shared wry looks at the thought of his dalliance with a girl a third his age.

Really, the only inexplicable element, in all the days of Michael Stuyvesant's passing, was the enormous man with the white beard who sat toward the back of the Episcopal cathedral during the funeral, shouting out his Amens, where the rest of the congregation murmured, and belting out the hymns in a strong and surprisingly good bass voice. He came to the gravesite as well, although no one seemed to know him and that smaller service was supposed to be only for family.

Strangest of all, when the service was over and Michael Stuyvesant had been carefully and gracefully lowered into his grave, the giant came over, shook the son's and daughter's hands, and left them with an envelope—before driving off in a beat-up old Chevrolet, with a loud rattle and belch of black smoke.

Inside the envelope was exactly $182.37 in bills and coins, and a months-old Minnesota hotel bill marked "Paid."

Port de Grâce

I

It was in the economy-sized car he had rented at the Duluth airport—a boxy sawed-off hatchback, like a truncated hearse—that Johnny Jasper decided he would be a stoic. A *Stoic*, with a capital S: a follower of the Ancient Roman philosophers; a self-contained man, unconcerned with what others thought or said of him.

The highway skirted the edge of Lake Superior, running north and a little east through a December landscape of pines and the occasional bare-limbed tree, its bright foliage fallen to leafmeal and blanketed with snow. Frozen hillocks and small lakes. A few stiff stone peaks. And a chill off the Great Lakes that left him feeling damp and cold. *Clammy*, Johnny thought. Hot and humid, down somewhere like Charleston or New Orleans, that's *muggy*. But cold and humid, like a crypt in a horror movie, that's *clammy*. That's Minnesota along the Superior shore.

The happiness of your life depends upon the quality of your thoughts, the car's speakers announced over the tinny whine of the heater's fan. "In this passage from his *Meditations*, Marcus Aurelius, the Stoic Roman emperor, is telling us to live inside ourselves. The more we care what others do, the less we are happy. *Think of the life you have lived until now as over and, as a dead man, see what's left as a bonus and live it according to Nature*, Marcus says. *Love only what happens and what is spun with the thread of your destiny. For what could be more fitting?*"

Johnny had subscribed to the podcast *The Strength Within: A Daily Dose of Stoicism to Make You Feel Good About Yourself* a few months earlier, having come across it in one of those rabbit-hole dives through the Web—the kind where one link leads to another, then another, then another until you finally look up from your computer screen to realize it's two in the morning and you will never reach the end of theories about how medieval monks brewed beer. Or arguments about which historical figures died the most gruesome deaths. Or explanations of why putting metal cans in microwaves is a bad idea.

For Johnny, the Stoicism dive had started with an attempt to identify a song that played over the ending credits of a ten-year-old television show he'd streamed one night. That led him to a lyrics site, where, eventually, he found the song's title. Which sent him to a video site, which offered a further link of an interview with the now long-broken-up band. Twelve and half minutes into the interview, the bass player mentioned that he'd been reading about Stoicism, which made Johnny search for the word, the results for which showed, as the second or third item, an ad for a podcast series offering a daily dose of the philosophy. And after a new-tab prowl through pages and pages of dubious and unsourced "inspirational quotations" from the Ancient Roman thinkers Epictetus, Seneca, and Marcus Aurelius, Johnny had clicked back to sign up for the daily Stoicism podcast.

Not that he actually listened to it every day. After the initial enthusiasm, he fell to every other day, then once a week. And recently the notices of new podcasts had remained unclicked, mute indictments in his email inbox. But when his friend Liz—Liz McCally, who'd been looking out for him since they were foster kids together in the group home—told him that the thief Bart Sagan needed someone to fly to Minnesota and retrieve a package, Johnny jumped at the chance, deciding he would use the trip to listen to the podcasts and make himself more stoical.

The package was heroin, Bart had told him once Liz had put them in touch. And it belonged to the mob-boss Harry King, which made things dangerous, and Johnny hesitated. Still, he decided, Bart was putting up the cash for the trip, and Johnny didn't have much planned for the Christmas season. Besides, this was his chance to show what he could do. Build a reputation as one of the good ones. Impress Liz, even. He pictured their quiet nods of appreciation when he brought back the package, acknowledging him as an equal, competent and successful.

Johnny was just starting to imagine the new jobs he'd be able to get when he noticed the speed limit dropping as he rounded a long curve on the highway. And there he was, at the city limits of Port de Grâce, Minnesota, on the afternoon of December 22, the noon sun already failing the day. *Founded by French voyageurs in 1802. Population 2,411*, the blue and white Chamber of Commerce welcome sign read. *Home of the Fighting Beavers of Superior County High School*, another panel added. *Division II state hockey champions!*

Easy as pie, Johnny decided. A quick in-and-out, and he'd be driving the 175 miles back to the airport in Duluth, heroin in his locked suitcase. All he had to do was park somewhere and hunt down the address Liz had given him. *Live as on a mountain. Let men see, let them know, a real man, who lives as he was meant to live. If they cannot endure him, let them kill him. For that is better than to live as most men do*, the Stoic podcast on Marcus Aurelius told him. And Johnny Jasper nodded. That's the ticket. That's the good stuff.

Finding the address turned out to be less easy than Johnny had supposed. The package had been sent to an Esther Eidolon at 310 Second, Suite 212. Along what seemed to be the town's main drag (called Coureur des Bois Street, for some unknown reason) he'd managed to fit his little car into what probably wasn't an actual parking place—a narrow diagonal slot next to a dirty pile of snow left by the winter plows, across from a motel and half a block down from some kind of fishing shop.

At least, that's what Johnny guessed from the mock-up of a fish tail, sticking fifteen feet into the air above the roof, and a ten-foot fish head, poking out of the side of the shop, as though an enormous trout had been rammed through the two-story wooden building. Its fishy eye glowered at him as he squeezed out of the hatchback. With a shiver, Johnny turned up the collar of his overcoat, sidled past the snow bank, and trudged the two blocks up to Second Street—where he found that the address didn't exist.

The missing place would have come between a café called Trout Haven—*Fresh Fish Fry Every Friday!*—and a small 1970s-style First Minnesota Bank, all yellowing glass and pockmarked concrete like a sprout of Tomorrowland, gone to seed. After walking up and down the block and double-checking the directions on his phone, Johnny decided to try his luck at the post office he'd passed.

"You're here to see the murals, I betcha. That's what strangers always come for. They're something special, I can tell ya. Painted during the Depression, when even artists were out of work. Let me just finish up with young Miss Meadows here, and I'll tell you all about them," a white-bearded man in a Postal Service sweater, raveling at the cuffs, called out from behind the wooden counter, his voice echoing from the tiles of the room.

And, sure enough, Johnny looked around to see two large murals, one above the counter and the other above the brass-door rental boxes that lined the wall behind him. Rendered in that clunky, large-limbed way of 1930s heroic-worker socialist realism, the first showed French voyageurs heroically loading their canoes, while the second depicted the wildlife of northern Minnesota: a heroic moose, some deer, a bear, and a trio of beavers busily bringing down a tree.

"Actually," Johnny said, turning back to the counter and away from the noble animals of the Great Lakes, "I'm a little lost and was hoping you could help me. When you're done with, um, the young lady, of course," he added, nodding to her, shapeless in her winter gear, as politely as he knew how.

She laughed, and Johnny noticed for the first time her bright eyes and the dirty-blonde hair framing a round, farmer-girl face. "You take care of him, Walter," she said. "You're the postmaster. I'm done here anyway, once I put stamps on these letters."

"Well, now, what seems to be the excitement that brings you on a cold December day to the historic Port de Grâce post office?" the postmaster asked, leaning forward to rest his elbows between the bric-a-brac on the counter: reindeer, candy canes, a North Pole workshop of busy elves overseen by a smiling Mrs. Claus.

"I, um, can't find an address I was given," Johnny tried to explain, finally pulling off his stocking cap and brushing back his matted hair to take a better look at the post-office pair. "It says 310 Second, in Port de Grâce, Minnesota."

"Second Street or Second Avenue?" Walter asked, winking at the woman.

"I, uh, don't understand. All I was given was just '310 Second.'"

Eventually, Johnny learned that in Port de Grâce the numbered streets running north-south were called *avenues*, while the ones running east-west were called *streets*. "So you get things like the corner of Third and Third. Confuses everyone, but it's too late to change. Things are what they are, and there's no sense crying over them," Walter added, nodding gravely at the philosophical wisdom of his pronouncement.

"So I'm looking for 310 Second Street, then?"

"Well, now, as postmaster, I'd have to tell you that 310 Second Street would be smack dab in the middle of the bank's parking lot, and I figure that probably isn't what you're looking for."

"Now, Walter, stop teasing the poor man from out of town," the young woman said, sliding her stamped envelopes into the outgoing mail slot and turning to Johnny. "I'm Sylvia, by the way. Sylvia Meadows. I'll walk you over to Second Avenue and Third Street. I have to stop by Larry and Pol's, anyway, to make sure about the Christmas flowers."

She took Johnny's arm, turning him toward the door and tugging him out of the building. Walter Berg—Port de Grâce postmaster for the past thirty years, and the man who knew just about everything about the town— pushed back his thin white hair and huffed in his beard. Not many strangers around in the winter. Hardly anyone to string along with a good long-winded joke, and then that young spark, Sylvia, had to go and steal the young man. Still, he was feeling too good to hold a grudge. The professional Santa the town council hired had canceled his gig, stuck in the huge snow-storm that had buried the southern half of the state, so Walter would finally get his chance to dress up and play the role at the Yule Tree Festival.

Out on the sidewalk, Sylvia let loose Johnny's arm to zip up her winter coat. "C'mon," she said. "It's just a few blocks this way. You didn't tell me your name, by the way, or what you're doing in town. Did you come for the Yule Tree Festival? It's not till tomorrow night, though, and you're not really dressed warmly enough for it."

She had that last part right, Johnny thought. His cloth overcoat was fine, even typical at home, he thought, but it just wasn't made for the icy damp cold on the freezing edge of Lake Superior. Parkas and snow pants. People here must have parkas and snow pants the way bankers have suits back east.

"I'm Johnny, um, I mean John. John Jasper. And I'm just in town to see someone for an hour or two before I head back to the airport."

"Well, Mr. Johnny or John-John Jasper, welcome to the Great North.

I think I'll call you John-John." She laughed again, and the steam of her breath glittered in the Minnesota sun.

Don't get distracted, Johnny told himself. *How much time he saves who does not look to see what his neighbor says or does or thinks*, Marcus Aurelius said. "Um, what's the Larry and Pol's you mentioned? Is it like a bar or restaurant?" he asked.

"No, no. I'm sorry. A local nickname. It's the Episcopal church, Saints Lawrence and Polycarp, just in the next block, across from the park. I promised to make sure the poinsettias had been delivered. And here you are, 310 Second Avenue." She tilted her head to give him a weighing look. "Come by the Trout, that's the place downtown, for dinner, if you're still in town. Around 6:00," she added and marched off up Second Avenue.

Turning away from the sight of Sylvia walking away in her padded snow clothes, like an overweight but toasty elf, Johnny Jasper saw the number *310* written in the mosaic tile of the foyer floor. It was an old Italianate office building with pointed windows and a heavy feel to the dirty red-brick façade. Only three stories high—as it needed to be, in the days before reliable elevators—it looked the kind of place where a *film noir* detective would have his office, a ceiling fan turning in the room and the transom window above the door cracked to let out the cigarette smoke and the rye-whiskey fumes.

Up the worn stairs, down the antique linoleum hallway, Johnny found Suite 212, the number and nothing else embossed in peeling gold leaf on the door's frosted-glass window. He could try to pick the old lock, he supposed (on a few late-night binges online, he'd watched some lock-picking videos, made supposedly to train locksmiths but actually to train thieves). Or, he figured, he could break out a corner of the window and reach in to unlock the door. Whatever people were on the floor seemed closeted in their own offices. But he could also hear his childhood friend Liz's voice telling him, *Try the handle first, doob*, and sure enough, the door was unlocked. He slipped into the office, carpeted in industrial gray, and shut the creaking door gently behind him.

A green steel desk, like something from a 1950s government tax office. Some scattered papers on the floor. A round metal wastepaper basket, dented and lying on its side. A pair of wobbly four-drawer filing cabinets. And dust on every surface. A pair of summer flies mummified on the cold windowsill beneath the venetian blinds. Johnny sat at the desk and gingerly opened the drawers, finding only more dust—until, in the center drawer, he saw a post-office slip filled out with a forwarding address. Which he shoved into his pocket when he saw shadows through the frosted window.

After some whispers out in the hall, like a muted argument about what to do, the handle rattled and the door swung open with a small screech of its unoiled hinges to reveal two men in dark parkas, their eyes snapping to him as he sat behind the desk. "Well, now, Damon, there seems to be a visitor here already," said the first, a slim-faced man with slicked back hair and a Middle Eastern cast to his features. "You aren't our friend Esther Eidolon, so what are you doing in her office?"

The second, a big man with twisted lips, added, "Yeah, that's a question, ain't it, Alastor?" He stepped around the first man and started looking through the filing cabinets. His partner turned the wastepaper basket upright and began picking up the scattered bits of paper on the floor, examining each before he dropped it in the basket.

So, they're Alastor and Damon, apparently, Johnny thought. He wasn't the best connected crook back home, never managing to be like Bart and Liz, who seemed to know everyone. But he could recognize the pair's basic types: a nasty jack-of-all-trades—the criminal world's equivalent of a utility infielder, if baseball players wouldn't mind knifing you—and his partner, a bruiser ready to break some heads.

"I'm looking for her because some friends back east need to get something she accidentally ended up with," Johnny offered carefully. He thought of himself as a reasonably tough guy. Nobody got through his city's foster-care without learning to fight. But he knew there wasn't much chance he could win against both of them, especially without the weapons the airport scanners forced him to leave at home. And he had caught the whiff of impending violence in the room, like stale cigarette butts in the ashtray the morning after. "Maybe you can tell me where this Esther Eidolon is, so I can talk to her."

"Now that's just what we going to ask you," Alastor said. He took out a lighter, a gold stick with a thumb wheel, and began clicking it over and over, with small puffs of flame popping up and cutting out, on and off, off and on. "You see, we don't know her, exactly, but we're in the same boat as you. Our friends in Minneapolis are anxious we should talk with her a little, just to find out, in a friendly way, what happened to the money she borrowed. But this Esther woman has been very hard to get ahold of."

"I just had this Second Avenue address," Johnny told them, "and it's the only place I've looked so far. Maybe we could look for her together, both get what we need."

"Now there's an idea. What do you think, Damon?"

The big man slid the last empty filing-cabinet drawer shut with a surprising gentleness. "Sounds like we got a partner," he said, his twisted mouth approximating a welcoming smile, although it didn't reach beyond his lips. "Where can we get a drink and talk about what comes next?"

II

Things of themselves have no hold on the mind, but stand motionless outside it, and all disturbances arise solely from the opinions within us, Johnny Jasper's podcast quoted as he parked at the Donut Hole diner the next day. *All that you presently behold will change in no time whatsoever and cease to exist.* "In this passage, the great Roman Stoic reminds us . . . " But at that point, Johnny Jasper turned off the ignition and popped open the flimsy car door. Easy enough for Marcus Aurelius, he thought. He didn't have to waste an entire morning waiting for Alastor and Damon, the loan-shark collectors from Minneapolis, to show up. He didn't have to phone his friend Liz McCally and explain why he didn't yet have the package he had flown to Minnesota to find.

Johnny hadn't slept well in his drafty room at the Timberland Lodge, the motel across from the giant bait-shop fish. A Lake Superior steelhead trout, he had unwillingly learned from a bartender the previous day, shaped to look like it was fighting a fishing line, and he could feel it keeping an eye on him all night through the crack in the motel curtains. Feel it watching him even now, late the next morning, when he'd given up on Alastor and Damon, and left the motel to find some food.

"Hiya!" the waitress chirped as Johnny gingerly lowered himself onto the red padded turntable of the lunch-counter stool. "You in town to see the alligator? It's pretty special. Came all the way down from Algonquin

Park, up in Ontario. One of the last northern alligators left. It'll be at the Yule Tree Festival tonight."

"Coffee," Johnny said, trying not to engage in any more local lore.

"You want anything, hun?" she asked, pulling out her pad.

"Coffee."

"Oh, right, you said that. Anything to eat?"

"Eggs, up. Bacon and toast."

"No juice?"

"No."

"Really? You should get your vitamins."

"No," he snapped, and she turned away in a huff.

But not for long. While his late breakfast was cooking, the rail-thin waitress leaned across the counter again and told him that *alligators* were what they called the old-fashioned timber boats that the logging companies had used: stream-driven side paddlers that could push floating carpets of logs along the rivers and lakes, and the paddle could be used as a winch to pull the tug across the land between the waters.

Eventually, though, the food came, portaged from the window into the café's kitchen. And as he pushed his egg yolks around the plate with triangles of toasted American-standard white bread, Johnny thought about the previous day. He hadn't found the package, but nothing bad had happened, exactly. It's just that, looking back, he felt uneasy, as though some heavy charge had been in the air. As though some sign had tried to make itself known, even while he kept missing it.

He still couldn't spot what was making him nervous. All he'd done was have a drink or two at Trout Haven with Alastor and Damon, as the daylight turned to early dark. And he'd ended up telling them about the Stoicism he was, well, *studying*, he'd said, although that was maybe a little inflated a description for listening to podcasts on the three-hour drive from Duluth to Port de Grâce. Alastor had argued with him a little, clicking his lighter on and off, like an ex-smoker needing a replacement habit, and said it was all too grim and death-obsessed. *Style*, that's what mattered. Maybe if they could add a little style, a little panache, to all that stuff about being brave and not caring about other people, then it might amount to something.

Even suspecting it was a mistake, Johnny had showed them the mail-forwarding form he'd found in Esther Eidolon's office, an address in a set of cabins, according to his phone's map app, miles out of town. And they'd agreed to meet him the next morning at his motel and travel with him out to the cabins. At least, he thought, he didn't tell them about Harry King and the three kilos of heroin that got accidently sent to Esther Eidolon. Just a drink or two in, and he found himself about to spill the whole story of the misdirected package. But just in time, a few minutes before 6:00, Sylvia came through the Trout Haven door, and Johnny stopped talking to stand up and wave to her.

"Not very stoic of you, is it? Meeting a girl," Damon tried to joke, though it came out as a sneer. Alastor quickly stood up and signaled the bruiser to do the same. "We'll leave you to your date and see you early tomorrow at the motel," he said with a unctuous attempt at grace. The pair wrapped themselves up—even gangsters in Minneapolis wear sensible parkas, with fake fur lining the hoods, Johnny noticed—and nodded to Sylvia, unwrapping herself from snow clothes near the door, as they headed out into the early dark.

As for the dinner itself, as Johnny looked back on it, he'd had a reasonably good time. The Trout Haven food was better than the typical bar food he would sometimes make the mistake of eating back home. Or at least the fish sandwich and fries he'd ordered on Sylvia's recommendation tasted fine. What was offered as salad proved to be a sad coleslaw, a mess of cabbage and carrot shavings that had drowned itself in runny mayonnaise and dissolved sugar. Maybe you couldn't get fresh vegetables in small-town Minnesota in the winter.

A little disturbed by how close he'd come to telling his new partners too much about the heroin and Harry King's business, Johnny decided to switch from beer to ginger ale for his meal with the local girl. She was good-looking, he decided, in a wholesome way that he wasn't used to: red-cheeked midwestern, with bobbed hair, an easy smile, and eyes sharper than her face should have.

"So," she said, "you aren't on the road back to Duluth."

"Yeah," Johnny answered. "Didn't finish up my work here yet."

"Well, my gain, I suppose. Or yours."

Laconic, Johnny decided. That's what he would be. Sylvia would appreciate a man of few words. And it would fit well with the Stoicism he was learning: *Concentrate every minute like a Roman,* as the podcast had told him, *on doing what's in front of you with precise and genuine seriousness, . . . freeing yourself from all other distractions.* Which didn't explain why, just half a sandwich later, he was telling Sylvia about Marcus Aurelius, and his childhood in foster homes with Liz McCally, and how much he wanted Bart Sagan to like him, and how clammy—yes, *clammy*, not *muggy*—it felt through a cloth overcoat on the shores of Lake Superior, and even how he was thinking maybe he should get himself a parka. You know, one of those waterproof-shell ones, with a thick lining and fur on the edges of the hood. With big pockets and a heavy-duty zipper.

And Sylvia laughed, at Johnny a little and then with Johnny a lot, as they made fun of the cold in northern Minnesota. And she told him about growing up in Port de Grâce, a proud graduate of Superior County High School and then Bemidji State University, over in the middle of the state, where she'd gotten a degree in computer web design, which is how she was supporting herself. She talked about how she tried to help out the townsfolk she'd grown up with, and how much she liked her Episcopal parish, the prettiest church in town. If he was still around the next night, he should come to the annual Yule Tree Festival, which is as close to a Christmas festival as old Mr. Gustavson—Bent Gustavson, the town atheist—would allow without driving down to Minneapolis to file suit against the town council for sponsoring a religious event.

It was when he caught himself staring into Sylvia's face, watching her sharp eyes and smile, that Johnny had realized he needed to shake loose. He paid the bill, wished her goodnight, and left to book a room at the Timberland Lodge—the motel watched by the unsleeping eye of the bait shop's giant steelhead trout. Maybe, he thought later that night, he'd come back for visit sometime. In the summer, when it was warm, and maybe look Sylvia up again.

But now, in the late-morning light of the next day, holding his coffee mug and staring down into it—avoiding eye contact with the chatty waitress who wanted to tell him about a house fire in town during the night and how dreamy the volunteer firefighters were—Johnny realized that he needed to figure out what to do. Give up on Alastor and Damon, he supposed, and handle things on his own.

Yep, that's the ticket, he decided. Leaving cash for his breakfast on the counter, he wrapped himself up as warmly as he could and braved the cold walk to the car. A ninety-mile drive on State Highway 1, his phone app told him, to something called Pine Roost—according to his search engine, a set of summer places out on the southern edge of the Boundary Waters Wilderness in Minnesota's Superior National Forest.

Cold enough to freeze a waterfall, is that a thing? Johnny didn't think he had ever seen before a frozen cascade, a jumble of irregular ice columns like baker's icing that had flowed in rivulets down the side of a cake and then hardened. A fantasy of ice sculpture in the twelve-foot drop from one frozen lake to another.

At least, Johnny supposed they were lakes. After eighty miles of northern Minnesota in December, he had decided that anything flat without trees was water. Hard to tell for sure, with everything blanketed in snow, but the pines were everywhere else, and what kept them from growing in the empty spots? *Time is a river, a violent current of events, glimpsed once and already carried past us, and another follows and is gone*, his Stoic podcast insisted as his map app told him to turn right on a barely plowed road between two gateposts.

Creeping on the compressed snow a few miles off the highway, into the woods, following the tracks of a previous car that had marked the road with a trail, Johnny came at last to a small enclave of log buildings. This, he thought, must be what summer houses looked like years ago: log-cabins with porches to sit on while the kids ran around among the trees, and rickety boathouse shelters for the canoes, and a dirt road for the drive back to town to pick up groceries.

All of the snow-covered cabins appeared deserted, with unshoveled entryways and wooden shutters like small barndoors over the windows. The only light he could see, the only thin tendril of fireplace smoke, was from what seemed to be the central lodge. Wrapped with two stories of timber-framed porches, screened against the summer mosquitoes breeding in the area's endless waters, a faded sign said *Pine Roost Lodge and General Store* in block letters.

The tires of the hatchback crunched in the snow as he pulled up in front. Leave the motor running, Johnny thought. I won't be long, and I'd

freeze to death if I couldn't get it started again this far from help. The exhaust puffed in small staccato coughs as Johnny got out of the car.

A figure in a long red stocking cap—dangling down the side of his face like Scrooge in a Victorian night cap or the French voyageurs with their knit toques in pictures around Port de Grâce—opened the lodge door and stepped out onto the porch. Wearing floppy, unbuckled rubber overshoes, his shoulders wrapped in a blanket. And a shotgun cradled in his arms, Johnny was unhappy to see. The thin, gray-haired, unshaven man looked Johnny up and down. "You here for the sarsaparilla?" he asked. "We're closed for the season, but I could maybe scare up a bottle you could take with you, if you've got the cash."

Turns out—as Johnny was forced to learn with the polite attention of someone being told a story by a man with a gun—homemade sarsaparilla was the tourist attraction of the Pine Roost Resort. A century back, a woman named Dorothea Bellwood had lived alone on the property, an unpopulated area the size of Rhode Island stretching around her in the National Wilderness. Canoers and hikers would stop to visit, and Dorothea, like some aging Girl of the Limberlost, would offer them her self-bottled soft drink, a sort of sarsaparilla made from local roots and vines. The result was a licoricey and bitter version of root beer, but the Bellwood brew started a fad. Or at least as much of a fad as an isolated northern Minnesota camp could support, and visitors would make a point to bring her groceries from town and return the sarsaparilla bottles so she could make more. And though she had finally passed away just a few decades back, attributing her longevity to the health benefits of her soft drink, the people to whom her nieces and nephews sold her land kept the drink alive, commissioning a bottling plant in Bemidji to make small runs of it, following Dorothea Bellwood's hand-written recipe.

Only after the story, sitting at a kitchen table with a red-checked plastic tablecloth stapled to it, did Calvin Finn, as the caretaker turned out to be named, relax enough to set down the shotgun, leaning it against the counter while he set a teakettle on the stove.

"Actually," said Johnny, "I'm not here for the sarsaparilla. I'm looking for a woman who was supposed to be here at Pine Roost. Her name is Esther. Esther Eidolon." And then he raised his arms above his head—saying as calmly as he could, "Whoa, whoa there, I was just asking"—as Calvin snatched up the shotgun again and poked it toward Johnny's chest.

"You one of them?"

"One of who?"

"One of them big-city, Minneapolis types. Tough guys, they thought. Hah, there's nothing tough like country tough. I showed them." He squinted at Johnny, the gun wobbling from side to side. "Nah, you're from out of state. You don't even have a parka."

The whistle of the kettle made him start, and Johnny decided he needed to a light a candle at Liz's church when he got home, in thanks that Calvin didn't accidentally squeeze the trigger.

"Alastor and Damon? A skinny guy with an attitude and a head-basher?"

"Yeah, sounds like them. Some heathen name or another." His eyes narrowed again. "So, you do know them."

"No. I mean, I only met them yesterday in Port de Grâce. They said they just wanted to talk to this Esther woman, too, but I didn't trust them." Johnny swallowed and tried again. "Listen," he said in as ingratiating a tone as he could manage, "I'm not here for trouble. Can I put my arms down?"

Calvin kept the shotgun aimed, more or less, at Johnny for a few moments more, then lowered it back down. "Yeah, damn thing is too heavy anyway, and that teakettle is about to drive me crazy."

"So," he added, turning off the stove and setting the kettle to the side, "if you ain't them, who are you?"

Johnny explained that a package he needed had been sent by mistake to this Esther Eidolon, and he'd found a forwarding address at her office in Port de Grâce. Only as he said it aloud did Johnny realize that the fact the postal form was in Esther's desk, and not filed with the post office, probably meant that she hadn't actually moved out to Pine Roost.

"Yeah, them Minneapolis boys said something about the lodge being an address for her, but they didn't say how they came by it. They showed up last night, about 8:00 or so. Friendly at first, but then the big one pulled a knife on me, made me look up her name in the files, while the skinny one watched. I figured they weren't the kind to leave witnesses, but when they pushed me out of the back office again, they didn't realize there was a gun underneath the counter. So I grabbed it and chased them out."

Calvin hawked and spit in the sink. "Damn-fool city folk, they didn't know that nobody keeps a shotgun loaded like that, out here in the country." He stopped. "But don't you think it's not loaded now," he warned Johnny, his eyes narrowing again.

"No, no, I'm not like that, and I just came to ask. No trouble. I'm only looking for the missing package and wouldn't hurt anyone."

"Yeah, I figured you for one of the good ones." He sat down and looked across the table in way that incongruously reminded Johnny of Sylvia Meadows's judging stare. "There must be a streak of bad in you, though, if you're trailing around with that pair of goons. Not much chance of redemption for the likes of them."

He looked away, staring out the window at the snowy pines. "There's a parcel of weakness in you, too, son. Everyone you meet can see it, and they'll take advantage. That, or try to fix you up like some cute puppy dog who's afraid of thunder." He laughed. "Women, for the most part. I've seen women do the damnedest things for a good-looking boy they think they can save."

Calvin reached to his left and pulled a pad and pencil off the sideboard. "According to the office records, this Esther Eidolon reserved a spot here at the end of the summer but never showed up. She had to give an address when she booked a cabin, and since those knife boys got it out of me, I figure it doesn't much matter if you have it, too." He tore off the top sheet of the small grocery-list pad and slid it across the table to Johnny. Twelfth Street in Port de Grâce, it read: 1220 Twelfth Street.

"But, son," Calvin added after a sigh, "You'd best find the hard place inside you, as quick as you can. You're no match for that pair, those Minneapolis boys, the way you are now. Try to find the line inside you, the solid wall that separates right from wrong and stops you from crossing over. That kind of good hardness, it's the only thing that makes a man worth a damn in the end."

A little more back and forth, and Johnny was carefully turning his car around in the cleared space in front of the lodge and driving back to town, a bottle of Bellwood Sarsaparilla on the passenger seat.

III

It was about 5:00 that afternoon that Sylvia spotted him, idly stirring a cup of tea, round and round and round, in a booth at the Donut Hole.

"Hey, John-John," she called. "What are you doing here? You decide to stay for the Yule Tree Festival?"

When he didn't respond, she crossed the room to him, setting on the table a wicker basket, like something for a picnic that didn't seem likely on a winter day. Johnny looked up to see her studying him, before his eyes snapped to the basket, which had begun to move, shaking a little on its own.

"Oh," she said. "Kittens. A pair of them. Mrs. Jarman found them on her porch today, abandoned by their mother, and she asked me to take

them to the animal shelter for her. She doesn't get out much, because of her lumbago. Hurts like the dickens in the cold months."

But Johnny had enough of local doings. He sighed and looked back down at his tea.

Concerned, Sylvia squeezed onto the bench across from him. "You okay, John-John? You don't look happy today. Come on, tell me about it."

And there in the Donut Hole, for no reason he could understand, Johnny told her about it. The whole story, except for the heroin. *Something* was all he said: Something belonging to Harry King, a crime lord back home, had gotten mislabeled and sent to an unknown woman named Esther Eidolon, at the Second Avenue address she had walked him to.

The anxiety of the past two days spilling over, Johnny described Esther's office, his finding the mail-forwarding form, and his encounter with Alastor and Damon, the men she had seen leaving Trout Haven when she arrived the night before. He told her about how the pair of Minneapolis loan-shark enforcers had gotten ahead of him, using the forwarding address he'd foolishly shown them. How they'd gone straight that night to visit Calvin Finn, threatening the old man till he gave them a new possible address for the missing woman.

By this time, Sylvia and Johnny each had a tortoiseshell kitten in their hands, putting a little water into a saucer on the table for them and wetting a finger with the coffee creamer for the kittens to lick off. And Johnny continued pouring out his story, telling Sylvia about going around noon to Pine Roost and meeting Calvin Finn. Hearing from him about Alastor and Damon's visit, and learning about Bellwood Sarsaparilla.

Sylvia had heard of the drink, she said, but never actually tasted it. So Johnny reached over onto the seat beside him and brought up the bottle he'd bought at Pine Roost. "Your Christmas present, Madam," he said, handing it to Sylvia with the mock reverence of a wine steward. She studied the sarsaparilla for a moment, then smiled at him and tucked it into the kittens' picnic basket.

"So, what happened then?" she asked.

"The information Calvin gave me meant I had a new clue about the package, so I drove back to town. Stopped by the motel for a minute and then went straight to the new address: 1220 Twelfth Street."

"But I know that address. Isn't that the house that . . . "

"Yep," Johnny said, watching the fierce kitten stalk his finger along the tabletop. "The house that burned down late last night. Alastor and Damon must have set it on fire, after they broke in." He looked down tiredly. "If she was home, they killed Esther Eidolon, too, or at least grabbed her and took her back to their boss in Minneapolis. And maybe they took what I'm looking for, as well."

He picked up the kitten and held it against his chest. "Though I guess it's more likely that they just burned up the package with the rest of the house, since they didn't know to look for it. And now I'm done. Nothing else to try. Those two are in the wind. The stuff I was sent to get is probably destroyed. All that's left is for me to call and tell my friends I failed."

"Oh, John-John. I'm sorry," Sylvia said, looking at his face. "No. Wait a minute. What did you say the woman's name was? The woman who got sent the package?"

"Eidolon. Esther Eidolon."

"Oh, John-John, you idiot. Why didn't you tell me before? I could have told you where her mail is. Walter Berg, the postmaster, could have told you." She laughed so hard she frightened her kitten and had to calm it against her own chest. "Just think, John-John. The first two people you met in town could have answered all your questions, if you had just said her name aloud."

She chortled again, and Johnny found himself starting to get angry. "You going to tell me, then? I mean, if you're done laughing at me."

Even as his face got tighter, Sylvia couldn't stop herself from pushing a little more. "Aren't you supposed to be a Stoic? You know, free from anger, patient, not caring when other people tease you?"

Johnny looked for a moment at his paw-waving kitten, trying to calm himself. He didn't know this midwestern woman. Not really. And at any point she could stop seeing his quest as an adventure she could join, and start seeing it as a crime she needed to tell the local sheriff about. He couldn't scare her away before she told him where the mail had gone. "*We all love ourselves more than other people, but care more about their opinion than our own,*" he said quietly. "A Stoic, Marcus Aurelius, wrote that. I was just a little sad that you were laughing at me, because . . . "—he twisted his mouth in a wry smile—"because I found myself caring about what you thought of me."

"John-John, that's . . . that's something to think about," Sylvia answered slowly, her face sobering as she looked at him. "Yes, that's something. And I'm sorry I laughed. It wasn't really at you, more at how absurd the situation is."

She took a sip from Johnny's untouched water glass, "So, anyway, the missing mail. It's all at the church. My church. Larry and Pol's."

"That can't be right. Why would it be there?"

"The pastor is a friend of hers, I think, or she's connected to the church in some way. And when I asked about the mail piling up in the vestry, he told me that he was letting her have her mail forwarded to the church while she was out of town." Sylvia widened her eyes. "Oh, John-John, think about it. If she's out of town, that means she almost certainly wasn't in that house on Twelfth Street that burned down. She's still alive."

Sylvia nodded decisively and began putting the kittens back in the picnic basket. "Let's go. We can look through the mail, see if your package is there, and then ask the pastor if you take it, or, at least, if he knows how to reach Esther Eidolon so you can ask her yourself."

She squeezed out of the booth in her parka and snow pants. "C'mon. We can go look for the package, then visit the Yule Tree Festival across the street. Julie from the animal shelter will be there, somewhere, and I can give her the kittens. Then we can eat."

Tugging at Johnny's arm to get him moving, Sylvia added, "Have you had lutefisk? Oh, or aebleskivers? They're like round Danish pancakes. The women from the Lutheran church always make them at the festival, and you have to try some."

Saints Lawrence and Polycarp, the Episcopalians' church in Port de Grâce, was made of wood—but wood assembled as though it were stone, as near as Johnny could tell: pointed-arch windows, steep gables, a square tower spire, and gingerbread trim. *Carpenter Gothic*, Sylvia proudly told him, maybe the finest example in the north country. When the nineteenth century's Gothic Revival reached these out-of-the-way American places, there wasn't enough money for stone, like the typical churches of the time in the big cities. What these small towns did have was lots of trees and lots of talented carpenters. So they looked at the architectural pattern books of those days and just cut wood to recreate it.

"You see," Sylvia explained, ushering him through the red door of the white church, "The Catholics were here first, with the French traders and voyageurs. And when the Scandinavian immigrants came, they built a Lutheran church for themselves. In other places, the Episcopalians typically built fancy English Gothic-style places, but here in the north we weren't as high class, so we built a Carpenter Gothic church from the Minnesota trees. My great-grandfather was pastor at the time, and he made it all happen."

Why the residents of Port de Grâce were so intent on telling him local lore, Johnny wasn't sure. People back east didn't do this, as far as he could remember, and there was so much more history in the big cities. Still, he had to admit, the inside had a formal old-fashioned beauty, with chestnut-stained wood arches and wainscoting, white-washed walls, and huge timbers carved into columns.

"Yep," Sylvia nodded as Johnny looked around the church. "That's our Larry and Pol's." She marched up the side aisle in her parka and snow pants. "C'mon," she said. "I'll show you where we're keeping the mail."

What she called the vestry turned out to be a small room to the right of the altar, holding a pair of old chests, a doorless closet with an empty hanging bar, and a long thin table against the wall. Sylvia set the kitten-filled picnic basket on the table and reached down to pull out a small cheap plastic bin, with "Property of the U.S. Postal Service" stenciled on the side. "And here we are," she said proudly. "Esther Eidolon's forwarded mail."

Johnny set the bin on the table and saw a bulge in the middle, covered with advertising flyers, out-of-date magazines, and utility bills. Holding his breath, he gently brushed away the loose mail to find a brown-paper-wrapped package with a return label from the shipping center that Bart Sagan had told him to look for. He smiled, for the first time in a day, and gently tore the wrapping paper to reveal a white box with a gold bow.

"Um, I don't think . . . ," Liz said, putting her hand on his arm. "I mean, we shouldn't just go ahead and open her mail. Now that we know it's here, let's go talk to the pastor."

But Johnny was already lifting the box lid. "I just need to make sure this is what I came for," he said. And sure enough, inside the box was a plastic bag wrapped securely with duct tape, containing three kilos—6.6 pounds—of Harry King's missing heroin. He lifted it up and held it for a moment, wondering why he wasn't feeling as quite as happy as he thought he would.

"Now isn't that a strange sight to see in a church, just before Christmas?" came a voice from the doorway. And Johnny sighed, as though it were something expected, some apprehension of malignant fate finally coming true. "Look, Damon," said Alastor, in that annoying voice that missed the sardonic his smirk suggested he thought he had achieved. "It's our stoical acquaintance and his girlfriend. I told you that if we followed them, we'd find out they knew more than they were saying."

"Yeah, you were right. I still think we should have just grabbed the guy and beaten it out of him, but here we are," the big bruiser Damon grumbled. "Maybe more interesting, though, is that bag he's holding."

"Right, the bag," agreed Alastor, pulling out a pistol. "Set it down on the table, why don't you, Johnny, and you and the girl just back over against the wall."

While Damon stood in the doorway, knife in hand to keep Johnny and Sylvia from escaping, Alastor pawed briefly through the bin of mail, then lifted the lid of the picnic basket. "Oh, look what our favorite couple is carrying around, Damon. Kittens in a basket. My heart almost melts at how cute they are." He started to reach in, but one of the frightened kittens scratched his finger. He jerked away and cursed, then slammed the lid shut. "Damn things. They should all be drowned."

"Enough fooling around," he said, turning to Johnny and Sylvia. "Tell us where Esther Eidolon is, why her mail's here in a church, and why you have a bag of what looks like drugs. Tell us, and maybe the two of you might get out of here alive."

"No noise," Damon warned him, gesturing with his head toward the door. Johnny could hear voices and tinny Christmas music, the sounds of the Yule Tree Festival starting up in the park across the street.

"Ah, right," Alastor agreed. "As my friend reminds me, we don't want to bother a whole lot of other people. So just tell us what we need to know." He paused for a moment, studying Johnny. "You don't have any style, but who can tell which way people will jump? You might get brave, all stoical, and hold back on me. So let me show you how serious we are."

Alastor took Sylvia's arm and pulled her away from Johnny. "Now, don't get excited. Just pay attention." And raising his gun, he slapped her across the head with the barrel. As she fell to the floor, he danced back a few steps, pointing the pistol back at Johnny to stop him from lunging at him. "Now, now. Just stay there. We'll hurt you and the girl until you explain everything. You really don't want to see what Damon can do with a knife."

And Johnny gave up. He told them about the misdirected package. He admitted it was three kilos of heroin, worth some real money, and he mentioned Harry King's name. He told the pair of Minneapolis enforcers that Esther Eidolon was gone, nobody knew where. And he explained how Sylvia, who helped out the church, knew her mail was being forward there.

But, in the end, even when doubled over after being slapped and taking a few body punches from Damon, Johnny didn't tell them that the pastor might know how to get in touch with Esther. He just couldn't bring that down on him. And he didn't tell them about Liz McCally and Bart Sagan, the thieves who had sent him on the Minnesota trip. Friendship, he thought, ought to count for something.

Alastor seemed to sense, in some irritated way, that Johnny was still holding out him. He reached down to grab Johnny's hair and lift up his head. "What are you not telling me? What's still inside that stupid noggin of yours?"

But Johnny only smiled through his bloody teeth and spit as hard as he could in the thug's face. With a curse, Alastor stepped back and cracked Johnny on the head with his pistol.

"Too much," Damon said, walking over to look at the body collapsed on the floor. "Why'd you have to hit him so hard? We won't get anything out of him now."

"Yeah, I know. I know. He just got me worked up." Alastor wiped his face with a handkerchief from his coat pocket. "This Eidolon woman is on the run, and I don't see any way to catch up with her." He pushed the cloth back into his pocket. "Still," he said, looking at the bag of Harry King's drugs, "we do have this heroin. I figure that's enough of a win while we let this town cool down and wait to see if she ever pops back up."

Damon growled a little, then nodded at Sylvia and Johnny. "What do we do about them? I don't want the cops coming after us, and they're still alive."

"It's a wooden building," Alastor said with a grin.

"I don't know what it is with you and fire," Damon grouched, but he turned away from the bodies and headed toward the vestry door. "Fine. Do your thing."

Johnny Jasper woke with a cough, if it could truly be called waking. He surged to his feet in panicked confusion, looking wildly around the room for his attackers, before melting back to the floor, moaning and holding his head.

It was just the smoke that woke him, he thought, feeling calmer as he saw that Alastor and Damon were gone. Just the smoke creeping under the vestry door, and the crackling noise coming from the church—and with that realization came a new thought: The church was on fire, and he and the pistol-whipped Sylvia, still unconscious on the floor, were trapped in a small room a long way from an exit.

He gathered himself and, twisting to put his hand on the floor, pushed himself slowly upright. He coughed again and felt a sharp pain in his side. A broken rib, he supposed. And light-headedness. A concussion? Probably, he thought. A sore jaw, too. He stumbled over to put his hand on the door, and, as he had guessed was likely, he could feel through it the heat of the burning church.

Johnny couldn't think of a time he had been in worse shape. At the same time, he noticed with a strange abstraction, he couldn't remember being so unconcerned. It was as though everything—his likely death from fire, even the pain of his own battered body—was happening outside himself. It mattered, of course, but didn't *really* matter. And he could see each step of what he needed to try with a calmness he had never known before.

Looking for something to cover his mouth and nose, he opened the chests in the room. One was stacked with old hymnals, but the other held flags. Johnny hadn't noticed flagstaffs on the front of the church, but he wouldn't complain. He draped the first, an American flag, around his head and tied it in a twist, the stars wrapping his head and the stripes hanging down to cover his neck.

He grabbed the second—an Episcopal church flag, although he didn't know it, with a large red cross in the center and a blue upper left quarter, dotted with small X-shaped crosses like miniature stars. Stumbling with the flag over to the vestry table, he opened the picnic basket. "Shhh, little guys," he said, gently pushing the kittens back and pulling out the bottle of Bellwood Sarsaparilla. "You just stay quiet in there. It will all be over soon."

Johnny cracked the bottle on the table edge, and the bottle cap and upper lip broke off neatly. "Huh, did you see that?" he asked the unmoving Sylvia. "As clean as a whistle. Not sure I could do that again in a thousand tries." He poured the sarsaparilla over the Episcopal flag, mopping up the excess to get it as wet as he could. Clear, he thought. Once you knew it probably wouldn't work, once you really saw that you were pretty sure to die, everything was easy. Clear. Laid out in obvious steps.

He knelt and pulled Sylvia up to drape over his shoulder. The weight almost brought him back down, with a mind-whitening flash of pain from his broken rib as he struggled to stand, but he made it to his feet and walked back to the table. He wrapped the wet flag to hang loose over his nose and mouth, and found himself looking at the picnic basket. "Oh, why not?" he said to Sylvia, and he hung the handle of the kittens' basket in the crook of his arm. Then he raised the wet flag to take a deep breath and opened the door, stumbling out into the church in the jog that was as close as he could come to a run.

Carpenter Gothic, Sylvia had called the nineteenth-century building, but all that meant to Johnny was that it was old wood, ready to burn. The pews, he noticed distractedly, were holding on against the fire, but the flames were on the walls, roaring up the stairs to the belfry, and engulfing the carved arches. Only a few feet near the floor were clear of smoke, which meant Sylvia's head was mostly in clean air, but Johnny couldn't get low enough to draw breath from it.

"Fire is really interesting, isn't it?" he tried to tell Sylvia, but it came out only as a choking rasp. The pretty orange flames licked the widows, beginning to melt the leading between the stained-glass pieces and consuming the plaques on the walls from the edges in, like paper browning from heat and curling in on itself. A beam crashed down behind him, the spray of sparks urging him forward before the building collapsed, but Johnny was already moving as fast as he could, one step after another as his strength ran out like hourglass sand.

He couldn't remember how he had reached the church doors, but even as his breath failed, he knew what came next. He shouldered open the door, the fire roaring up behind him with the influx of new air, and lurched out to the top of the stone stairs outside the church.

A semi-circle of people were watching the church fire. The volunteer fire department, uncoiling their hoses. The revelers from the Yule Tree Festival. Walter Berg, dressed in a homemade Santa suit. The bartender from Trout Haven and the waitress from the Donut Hole. All turning to look in a silent moment, the flashes of dozens of cell-phone cameras focused on the figure emerging from the church.

And there Johnny Jasper stood. The American flag over his head, and the Episcopal flag's cross hanging down from his face. On his shoulder, a rescued woman, and on his arm a basket of saved kittens, one of them poking its triangular face out of the wicker basket just in time to complete the picture.

Watch the movements of the stars as if you were running with them, and let your mind constantly dwell on the motions of the heavens, for such thoughts wash away the dust of life, he almost remembered from Marcus Aurelius. "The stars are beautiful," he tried to mumble, before dropping slowly to his knees and then to his side, Sylvia Meadows on top of him.

IV

Recovery from third-degree burns and deep smoke inhalation is never certain, especially for someone already as injured as Johnny Jasper had been after his beating in the church vestry. Sylvia's concussion was serious enough to put her in a hospital bed for a few days, but she had less smoke damage, and her parka and snow pants had kept most of the sparks off her. Johnny's prognosis, however, was doubtful, even after he had been airlifted to a famous university hospital in Minneapolis—where they had taken him because where else do you take a hero? A man brave enough to rescue women and kittens, with the style to do it just before Christmas, in a church, wearing an American flag and a red cross? Even Minnesotans understood that.

And, in fact, Johnny didn't die. Some fate, some watching angel, intruded enough to see him back on his feet, gingerly, after three or four weeks, ready to leave the hospital for outpatient therapy. Unconscious for the first few days, he had missed the media frenzy about his heroism. Dozens of pictures of him—but especially one with a kitten looking over the edge of the basket on his arm—had been slathered across the internet, the feel-good story of the week making the pages of newspapers, and the screens of television news shows, across the country. Fortunately for the heroic effect, his face wasn't disfigured, protected from the fire just enough by the sarsaparilla-soaked flag.

Caving to the pressure, the hospital finally convinced him to see a local Minneapolis newspaper reporter and a television personality from a national morning-show—a beautiful woman with a smile that didn't seem to move with her face. Johnny gave them the story he had concocted to explain his presence in Port de Grâce. Ice-fishing, he said. When they asked about how he would use his new fame, however, he wanted to snap, *When you've done well and another has benefited by it, why like a fool do you look for a third thing on top—credit for the good deed?* But he only faked a smile and pretended that he was too hoarse to continue.

He spoke with Liz McCally most days, on the phone she'd had delivered to the hospital since his own had melted. She had wanted to come out and be with him, but he talked her out of it. He needed to be alone, figure himself out, before he was ready. Still, he was glad to learn that the lost package didn't matter, with Bart Sagan flown away somewhere safe after ruining and bankrupting the drug lord, Harry King, and no one coming after Liz. She was the one who collected all his press notices, reading them to him over the phone and laughing. Neither of them could decide what he should do when he had recovered.

A few visitors stood out to him over the tedious days, although he couldn't quite say why. The first was a pregnant teenager—elfin, with a fox-like face—in a hospital gown. At the beginning, while they were keeping his room sterile and no visitors were allowed, she had watched him through the window. When he noticed her and gave a bandaged wave, she laughed and waved back, bobbing excitedly on her toes.

Later, when he was allowed visitors, she stopped by to sit with him, a chatty girl with some fading bruises. Cheyenne, she said her name was, in the hospital for observation of her pregnancy. "I'm getting out tomorrow, though. Isn't that something? But I wanted to come down to your room first, just to find out what makes someone a hero. I know another man who's maybe a hero, but he's gone back home now."

Johnny laughed and told her he didn't know. Maybe nobody did. You just have to be brave, try to do what was necessary, and sometimes the moment comes along, all by itself.

The second visitor he noticed, or thought he did, was a tall, thin woman with a stern face, long-fingered hands, and skin so pale it seemed almost ethereal. He could have sworn he saw her watching him as he slept, once or twice, but she always slipped out before he was fully awake. With no evidence, Johnny decided that she was Esther Eidolon, checking up on him. He half expected Alastor and Damon to come finish the job on him, but with the manhunt combing the state for the pair, they must have had the sense to run far away.

His final visitor came as he was checking out, pushed along in the mandatory wheelchair toward the hospital doors: Sylvia Meadows, standing there in the lobby, watching him, her hands on her hips.

"Hello," he said, squinting at the figure backlit by the winter light through the plate-glass windows. "Were you looking for me?"

"The nurse on your floor wasn't supposed to say, but she knew I was the one you carried out of the fire, and she called to tell me when you were being released today." She eased the weak man up out of his wheelchair and out the doors into the Minnesota cold. "And I thought I better drive down and help get you to a hotel while you figure out what comes next. Maybe buy some new clothes," Sylvia said as she guided him to her car. "You still don't have a parka."

And Johnny Jasper decided just to allow the river of events to flow where it would—the fabric of time to find its proper shape, woven from whatever threads of destiny this strange world had spun for him.

Part Two
Twelve Christmas Thoughts

Dakota Christmas

Late afternoon on Christmas Eve, the year I was eleven, my father took me with him across the river. I can't remember exactly what the hurry was, but he was a busy lawyer, and he needed some papers signed by a rancher who lived on the other side of the Missouri. So off we headed, west across the bridge from Pierre and north through the river hills.

If you've never seen that South Dakota country in winter, you have no idea how desolate land can be. I once asked my grandmother why her family had decided to stop their wagon trek in what became the prairie town where she was born. And she answered, in surprise I didn't know, "Because that's where the tree was." The tree. The empty hills were frozen dry, as my father and I drove along, with sharp ice crystals blowing up from the knots of cold, gray grass.

Now, we were supposed to stay for only a minute or two, get a signature, and turn back for home. But you can't pay a visit in South Dakota, especially at Christmastime, without facing food—endless besieging armies of it, and usually the worst of American holiday cuisine: Jell-O molds with carrot shavings, chocolate-packet pies, neon-pink hams pricked to death with cloves and drowned in honey. If you've never seen one of those prairie tables, you have no idea how desolate food can be.

From the moment she spotted us turning off the highway, Mrs. Harmon must have been piling her kitchen table with hospitality. I remember eating cinnamon buns crusted with sugar, sitting on a bench, while Mr. Harmon and his two tall sons told us about the coyote tracks they'd found that morning. It was the cold that made the coyotes risk it, scenting the trash cans, probably, and the livestock had been skittish all day. But then Mrs. Harmon began to shout, "Jim, Jim, the horses are out." And in a tangle of arms and jackets, we poured out to herd back the frightened animals.

By the time we were done, however, four expensive quarter-horses were loose on the prairie. Cursing, Mr. Harmon climbed into his pickup and headed north along the highway, while my father drove off to the south. Mrs. Harmon took it more calmly. She went inside to telephone the neighbors, and the boys began to saddle three horses to ride out and look.

You have to understand the significance of that third horse, for it marks the difference between town and country—even a small town surrounded by country, like Pierre. The Harmons simply assumed an eleven-year-old boy was old enough to help, while my mother would have pitched a fit at the idea of my riding out on the prairie, a few hours from sundown, in the middle of winter.

In fact, there was little chance of getting lost. I knew, more or less, how to ride, and the highway was in sight much of time. Still, as the land grew colder and darker, the excitement faded, leaving only brittle determination, a boy's will not to be the first to turn back.

I can't have ridden far through the Christmas hills—maybe three or four miles—when I came over a rise and spotted one of the horses, skittering in front of a worn farmhouse. Standing in the yard was a woman, a rope in one hand and her other hand held up empty toward the horse. She was hatless and tiny, hardly bigger than I was, with a man's heavy riding coat hanging down below her knees, the sleeves turned back to show the faded lining, and she seemed very old to me. Yellow light streamed out on the cold ground from the one lit window of the house.

As I rode down, she waved me back, talking to the horse in the gentlest, lightest patter, as though nothing much had ever been wrong, really, and, anyway, everything was all right now. He bobbed back and forth, nearer and nearer, until he touched her open hand with his steaming nose and she eased the loop over his neck.

"Bea Harmon called," she said, handing me the rope, "and told me you were all out looking for this boy. They often come to me, you know. He'll go along quietly now."

Her eyes were quick and black. "I don't see many people, here about," she chirruped, like a winter bird. "Come in and get warm. I'll make some coffee. No, you're a little young for coffee. I'll put some water on for tea, and there're the cookies I made in case someone came by." But I was proud of bringing back one of the strays and wouldn't wait. I shied away from her outstretched hand and galloped back.

Sometimes you catch sight of a turn, heading off into the distance—a dirt track or a county road at right angles to the highway, as you drive along those straight, miles-long lines you find only in the West. And you know you'll never go up it, never come back to find where it leads, and always there remains a sense, as you roll past, that maybe this time you should have turned and followed that track up into the distant hills.

Her hair was the same thin shade of gray as the weather-beaten pickets of the fence around her frozen garden. She had a way with horses, and she was alone on Christmas Eve. There is little in my life I regret as much as that I would not stay for just one cookie, just one cup of tea.

Joyous Surrender

I love the elegant Christmas-dining pictures in *Bon Appétit*. The holiday dishes and cutlery in the pricey Williams-Sonoma catalogue. The winter ornaments and widgets arranged so beautifully by Restoration Hardware. The season's advertisements in the *New Yorker*, the Sunday *New York Times* magazine, *House Beautiful*, and all the rest—clean, refined, sophisticatedly simple expressions of upper-middle-class taste, displayed in magazines for the rest of the middle class to gaze at in wonder. To aspire to in hope. To ache for in greed.

Not that I'm without the good old American impulse to ape the decorating manners of my betters. I can page through the exquisite pictures of *Architectural Digest*, unfazed by such photo captions as "A Dolce & Gabbana-designed Christmas tree shimmers in the Art Deco lobby of London's Claridge's hotel." But mostly I love all the magazine pictures of elegance, this time of year, because they help me grasp the deep, true meaning of the Nativity—since whatever Christmas is, it ain't this stuff. Oh, Santa Baby, it ain't this stuff, at all.

Give me the vulgarity of inflated reindeer, bobbing out on the lawn. Give me trees drooping under the weight of their ornaments. Give me snow piled to the rafters, the dozen crèches scattered wildly around the house, like breadcrumbs leading back through the woods. Give me homes so lit up that the neighbors dream at night of sunstroke. Fruit cakes so dense they threaten to develop their own black-hole event horizons. Gingerbread cottages and Mouse King nutcrackers and wreaths on every door and silly Christmas cards and eggnog so nutmegged that the schoolchildren carolers cough and sputter as they try manfully to gulp it down.

Tastefulness is just small-mindedness, pretending to be art. And Christmas isn't tasteful, isn't simple, isn't clean, isn't elegant. Give me the tacky and the exuberant and the wild, to represent the impossibly boisterous *fact* that God has intruded in this world. Give me churches thick with incense and green with pine-tree boughs, the approach to the altar that feels like running an obstacle course through the poinsettias, and a roar from the bell towers so ground-shaking that not even the deaf can sleep in.

A follower once asked St. Francis—oh, so prissily—whether it was licit to eat meat on the Feast of Christmas, and he shouted in reply, "On a day like this, even the walls eat meat. And if they cannot, then let them be spread with meat." Now there's a picture that won't make *House Beautiful* any time soon: the walls of the dining room dripping with smeared meat. Such an image will not be subsumed by any attempt to tidy up the holiday and make Christmas manageable. St. Francis points toward something about the wonder and the mess of the Incarnation: the shattering of ordinary life that the Nativity declares. The smash of predictability, the breaking of attempts at elegant organization. This world is out of our control—not just in the bad sense of sin and fallen nature, but also in the impossibly good sense that God, in his providence, has taken it in hand.

In other words, embrace the madness of the season. Bellow out the off-key carols. Smile at the silly reindeer. Empty your pockets into the Salvation Army kettles as the Santas ring their bells. Slip on icy walks with your arms full of presents. Load the tree with lights. Pray not in despair or supplication but in wild thankfulness. *Rejoice and be merry, set sorrow aside. / Christ Jesus our Savior was born on this tide.*

I have a friend whose outrage at the commercialized falsity of modern Christmas has led him to turn his back on much of the way the culture celebrates the season. A deep believer—a young mystic who has chosen to live his life very simply—he goes out every December to find a small branch, a fallen leafless stick, for Christmas. He stands it up in a pot on his table, decorates it with a handmade ornament or two, and sets a paper star on top. One year, he added a few pieces of popcorn strung on a thread, but I think he thought them a disruption, for they were gone the next Christmas.

This friend is probably a better Christian than I am, and he's certainly a better man. It's the hard center of the holiday that he wants not to be distracted from. He loves the discipline of Advent, because the Church's prayerful run-up to Christmas focuses his thoughts and prayers on the great gift of that holy time: on God's descending in the flesh, on the Blessed Virgin's assent to the celestial purpose, and on the beginning and the end of things, the Alpha and the Omega that is Christ. He tries to ignore, as best he can, the overblown, overexcited cheapening of Christmas in the loud

blare of the season, since it only makes him sad—or angry, or crazy, or depressed, or something; distracted, at any rate—to see that fundamental moment, when the divine appeared in human form, smothered under layers of phony "Happy Holidays!" cheer.

And it's true that I envy, in many ways, the intentionally minimal, prayerful life my friend lives. For that matter, his Christmas reaction—his angry distaste for the snake oil of the commercialized season—is surely intelligible, deeply considered, and strongly felt. I know just what he means.

I also know that he's dead wrong. My friend shares something that's present in the elegant, tastefully secular version of the holiday so beloved by upscale magazines, for they both betray a dislike of the vulgarity and impropriety of the culture's celebration.

But surely the point is that Christmas will never be *tame* (as C.S. Lewis might have put it). God can turn even secularized reindeer and snowflake decorations to his purpose. To reject them is to miss some of the ways in which the modern holiday follows the pattern of a messy medieval festival. It's to miss, for that matter, some of the ways in which human beings respond to the rich, abundant experience of God. When we see the busy sidewalks—when we're buffeted by the shoppers hurrying past the tricked-up Christmas decorations on the storefronts—we shouldn't imagine we're watching people who are smothering the impulse of religion. These are ordinary folk, trying to celebrate the season. They sometimes falter, as we all do, and they're often confused, as we all are. But they nonetheless grasp in a profound way that a real thing comes toward us in December, and they layer it over with whatever fake or genuine finery they can find—not to hide it but to honor it.

Besides, if you set yourself against the season, you're not going to win. So why not simply be pleased about it all? Smear the walls with meat—*carne*, the root of *incarnation*—if that's what it takes. Break out into song, if you want. Break out into sentimentality, if you can stand it. Break out into extravagance and vulgarity and the gimcrack Christmas doodads and the branches breaking under the weight of their ornaments. Break out into charity and goodwill. But however you do it, just break out. What other response could we have to the joyous news of the Nativity that God has *broken in*, smashing the ordinary world by descending in the flesh?

The Cold City

There was a woman screaming on Park Avenue—flecks of saliva spraying from her mouth as she raged into her cell phone, "It's not my fault." Over and over, like the squeal of a saw cutting bricks: *It's not my fault* and a run of foul names. *It's not my fault* and another run of names. *It's not my fault, you [bleep]ing [bleep]. It's not my fault, you evil [bleep]. It's . . . not . . . my . . . fault.*

I don't know, maybe whatever it was, it really wasn't her fault. But her cell phone and makeup, her dark purse and blue coat, warm leather gloves—the accoutrements of public sanity around that face of private madness—made her seem guilty. Guilty of *something*, down to the bone. The man at the Salvation Army kettle kept his tense back turned against her as he rang his Christmas bell. The crowds of passing strangers fixed their eyes at awkward angles and hurried by. A child stared anxiously till his mother began chattering about breakfast, overbright and overloud, as she tugged him around the corner.

I saw the screeching woman for a moment framed by the candy canes and white Christmas garlands soaped on the window of the storefront behind her. Then the traffic light changed, and I crossed the street, my shoulders hunched in self-protection. *It's not my fault, you evil [bleep]. It's . . . not . . . my . . . fault.*

Is twice a warning or only a coincidence? For I heard the phrase again that same day, in the vestibule of the bank after work. New York is still one of the world's great Christmas towns. Too dirty to clean up well just for the holidays, Manhattan still makes a brave show for the season. The shop-window mannequins sport their Christmas finery, and the railings on the apartment buildings don their strings of lights and tinsel. Maybe movies—from

Miracle on 34th Street on—are what have made New York's Christmases seem so iconic: ice skating at Rockefeller Center, skimpy elf costumes on the strutting Rockettes at Radio City, sleigh bells on the horse cabs, piles of toys at FAO Schwarz. The expensive window displays at the stores along Park Avenue.

But at least New York still tries, where many other cities seem to have given up. There in the bank, while I waited in line for an automatic-teller machine, I watched the New York shoppers hurry past, their arms full of Christmas packages, and listened to a man talking on his cell phone, one foot up on the window sill.

"It's not my fault," he explained in a confident boom. "I'm just the kind of person who has to keep after things." What is it about self-justification that always makes it seem so false? About that phrase "I'm the kind of person" that always makes it sound like the beginning of a lie? He was well dressed in loafers and slacks, a nice overcoat, and apparently indifferent to the fact that the people at the ATMs could overhear him. With the effortless patter of a story told many times before—with the sort of smooth charm that usually fails because it announces too openly just how charming it is trying to be—he launched into a long story about how he didn't really want to sue, but then he was just the kind of person who needed to see that he got his rights, and it wasn't his fault everything got so screwed up.

It's not my fault—the cry we've made every day since Adam took the apple. Down somewhere in the belly, there's an awareness of just how wrong the world is, how fallen and broken and incomplete. This is the guilty knowledge, the failure of innocence, against which we snarl and rage: That's just the way things are. There's nothing I can do. I wasn't the one who started fighting. It's not my fault. What would genuine innocence look like if it ever came into the world? I know the answer my faith calls me to believe: like a child born in a cattle shed. But to understand why that is an answer, to see it clearly, we are also compelled to know our guilt for the world, to feel it all the way to the bottom.

I sometimes wonder to whom all the city's cell-phone talkers are talking. People all around them, thousands and thousands: *there*, that angry balding man slamming past in his stained parka, and *there*, that coatless woman with the deliberately unfocused stare smokers wear as they stand with their arms crossed outside restaurants, and *there*, that tired-looking girl in the sweater trying to stop a taxi, and *there*, and *there*, and *there*—an endless stream of presence, and still they shout or murmur on the street, pouring secrets and imprecations into their clenched phones and ear-piece microphones. Talking to the ones who aren't there. Communing with the missing, like fortune-tellers with a crystal ball. Like mediums calling the dead.

Sometimes New York hints at something different. There is a strange impression the city gives after a snowstorm—a kind of small epiphany, a sense of being taken for a moment out of time. People walk down the middle of the streets. A few pull out their skis and slalom along First Avenue. The taxis all disappear, and for a moment the whitewashed city looks clean and small-townish.

But New York cannot play for long at being the New Jerusalem. The ultimate time-bound place, it cannot step far outside the rush and rattle of commerce. The City of Man, it cannot maintain its pose as the City of God. With their town bright and almost pretty in the snow, New Yorkers act for a few moments as though things have changed—or rather, as though these few moments don't count, as though the apocalypse of falling whiteness has lifted them out of time and left them for an instant clean and un-hurried. Last winter, I saw an old-fashioned toboggan—eight or ten feet long, the wooden slats curling to a swoosh in front—being drawn along Fourteenth Street, filled with laughing children. Who has room to store a toboggan in Manhattan on the off-chance of snow? Someone, clearly. Someone who has been waiting years for this white apocalypse.

Most Christmases, however, there are only cold drizzles, the icy rain that never seems to wash anything clean. I emptied my pockets on the way home from the bank: another Salvation Army kettle, a drunk man on the sidewalk with a hand-lettered sign I couldn't read, a woman rattling change in a paper cup. I hate the city, all tarted up in its Christmas clothes. Mewing us together on its streets, it forces us to see the human stain. It forces us to know. *It's not my fault*, I muttered as I blew on my cold hands. May God have mercy on us all. *It's . . . not . . . my . . . fault.*

Oh, Tinsel

Tinsel. No one needs tinsel. Even the word is a tinselly kind of word. It ought to have been a mild profanity, suitable for bridge clubs and 1950s sorority girls: "Oh, tinsel, I forgot my keys again, Janie." Instead, it names one of the most destructive substances known to humankind. Originally made from lead foil—till somebody finally noticed that it was turning children's livers purple and green—the loathsome stuff evolved through various aluminum incarnations to become the plastic killer that it is today. Tinsel murdered my vacuum cleaner this Christmas. Sucked up into the air vents, tinsel wrapped itself around the motor, melted, and smothered the helpless appliance. Tinsel smoked, and tinsel sparked, and tinsel set off the fire alarm. And now, on top of all the other holiday expenses, I have to run out and buy a new vacuum cleaner. Oh . . . tinsel.

I should probably pick up more wrapping paper while I'm out. There's never enough of the stuff. Has anyone else noticed something sick, something slightly disturbed, about wrapping paper? It's a neurosis, really: this desire to grab anything that isn't moving and swaddle it in oddly printed sheets of red and green. A genuine case of hebephrenia, I think, but I can't be sure because my reference books have all been shoved back on their shelves to make room for the piles of tissue paper, rolls of bright ribbons, and endless tubes of wrapping paper.

My wife and daughter are both mad wrappers. They love the whole panoply of Christmas coverings. They box, bedeck, and bundle. They camouflage, cloak, and case. They drape, enfold, mask, muffle, pack, sheathe, shroud, and veil. There's my daughter, happy as a bird, perched at the dining-room table, hand-coloring paper to wrap the hand-painted box that holds the hand-made present she prepared for her great-grandmother. The tip of her tongue sneaks to the corner of her mouth in her concentration, and she hums with the carols she's put on the CD player to help her along.

It's cute as a button, I know, but I still don't get it. I mean, nearly every purchased gift comes pre-packaged from the manufacturer in plastic and brightly printed cardboard, or nestled in a nice little box, and usually shrink-wrapped as well. And as soon as we buy it, we immediately clothe it in yet more layers of extraneous material: cotton batting, and tissue paper, and wraps, and boxes, and containers. My daughter spent weeks working on her presents—and now weeks more working on their wrapping, abetted by her mother: "I know, honey! Let's pack your aunts' presents in tissue paper and put them inside these nice little bags with the string handles! That way you can paint Christmas designs on the bags, too!"

Oh, goody. The mailman just brought the annual package from friends in Wyoming. Why do we have to open it? We know what it is. There's the brown grocery-bag paper, which covers the corrugated-cardboard box, which contains the Styrofoam peanuts, which bury the red and green wrapping paper, which surrounds the tin cookie box, which holds the sheets of wax paper, which envelop the homemade sugar cookies. The same homemade sugar cookies our friends send every year. All of which will be broken, because sugar cookies just don't travel well. I think I would have preferred a tasteful card.

And don't get me started on those padded envelopes filled with recycled lint. For several years now, these insufferable things have been the package of choice for small breakables at Christmas time. Perhaps they work better than the alternative, but mostly they seem to exist to spray gray dust and clumps of dryer fluff across the living-room carpet.

Ah, well. Christmas comes like a fire every year—a burning declaration of warmth and brightness in the December cold and dark. It's a stance, really, for Christians, a theological choosing of sides: Against the fall, God gave us *this*, and with *this* we will stand. Why should it be a surprise that the theology has psychological consequences? A preference for bright colors, a wish to decorate and adorn, a hunger for extravagance, a desire for celebration.

On Christmas Day, after Mass, I'll see the tree all gussied up, a bandits' den of brightly colored gifts underneath it. I'll watch my daughter open her presents—gently and carefully, not wanting to tear the pretty wrappings. I'll smell the Christmas dinner beginning in the kitchen and hear the Christmas music play. I'll look around in satisfaction at the wild mess of wrapping paper and opened packages and stray pine needles and scattered crumbs of sugar cookies. And I'll remember that I forgot to buy the new vacuum cleaner to clean it all up. Oh, tinsel.

Angels I Have Heard on High

I hear the angels, high in the hills. Up among the trees, the ponderosa pine and Black Hills spruce. Down through the snow-patched meadows, the counterpanes of brush and rock and long stems of cold, brown grass, forlorn above the ice. I hear the angel voices in the overtones of the wind through the buffalo gaps. I hear them along the frozen streambeds winding through the needles, down from the mountains. I hear them proclaiming the advent of the Lord.

In a sense, of course, to talk of angels in the wind is simply to construct an allegory. It's a way of saying that, if we are willing to be reminded, even the sound of the wind can make us think of the first Christmas, when the angels spoke to shepherds outside Bethlehem. Our days are thick with such reminders, if we pay attention; our lives filled with occasions for remembrance. Think just of the seasons: *The world is witness. It whispers holy things / of nature fallen and new grace that springs.* So why not hear a little bit of Christmas in the wind? The more we are willing to be prompted, the more this world seems redolent of the divine—even our senses overwhelmed. Our daylight thoughts. Our numinous dreams.

And amen to that pious prayer. Yes, always yes, to cries for recollection of the Christmas story. I love the Santas with their bells, the Salvation Army's call to charity on the sidewalks of America's cities. I love the stores with displays of candy canes and sleigh bells. I love even the Muzaked carols in the elevators, and the municipal trees, and the oversweet candies from the neighbors, and the fruit cake like depleted uranium, and the schoolchildren's nativity plays, and the Advent calendars, and the trips to the Food Bank, and the season's goose. For Christ's sake, why not be happy? So much around us shouts reminders of the cause for Christmas joy.

But I also mean something more than allegory here. Something more than pious metaphor and the familiar cheer of the season. I mean that celestial sounds were genuinely flowing down across a snowy field, just a few days ago. I mean that this December, here in the Black Hills of South Dakota, up in the highest registers of hearing, the clamor of heavenly voices really could be heard. I mean that the actual angels were actually here, actually singing tidings of great joy, and I actually heard them. I was not just reminded of the Bible stories of angels coming to Zacharias, to Mary—to shepherds, singing, "Glory to God in the highest, and good will toward men." I was allowed to understand, for a moment, a little of the great secret: The supernatural presses on the ordinary universe, straining to break through, and for a moment the world was changed. Charged. Made different, strange, and new.

I think some vague intuition of that secret is why I have always loved Christmas. This is the reason to embrace the madness of the holiday. The reason to surrender to the thousand crèches, the lighted decorations, the secular reindeer, the commercialized gift-giving.

Are they ideal? No, but little on earth is, and the almost medieval-like festival of modern Christmas serves, at least, to thin the barrier between this world and the next. The sappiest of Christmas carols have their purpose; the gooiest of Christmas movies have their point. I appreciate the theological density of "O Come, O Come, Emmanuel," patterning out the season's Festival of Lessons and Carols, but I can joyously (and tunelessly) howl along with the absurdity of "The Little Drummer Boy" and find tears in my eyes listening to "I Saw Three Ships." Even the manic silliness and sentimentality of the season work to God's intention. In the emotional storm and the blizzard of Christmas symbols, we open the little mystic gaps through which the angels slip.

A sinner—corrupt and soulsick, heartsore and muddled in my thoughts—I sometimes wonder what this world looks like to the saints. The universe must glow, every day a holiday, a holy day, like the blinding sunlight off clean snow and sharp swirls of sparkling ice. But it needs no individual grace, no special sanctity, to feel the life of the Christmas season. Portions of the wall are tumbling down, and through the breaches anyone can discern some of what we ordinarily keep hidden from ourselves: Christ himself in the faces of the poor and battered. The treasures that charity lays up in heaven. The supernatural beauty of nature. The joy of creation in the objects all around us. The almost sacramentality of everything real.

This December, I heard the angels singing. Actually heard their voices high in the wind, across a western meadow frozen stiff and covered with the fallen snow. Listen, and you'll hear them, too—down from the hills and the cold trees, ponderosa pine and Black Hills spruce. Along the icy streambed, through the brush, and over the rocks. All those voices caroling, praising, rejoicing: a swirl of joy beyond all deserving.

Beyond the Bleak Midwinter

Maybe you have to live in the bleak midwinter to get it. Maybe you have to see the countryside in its ash-white purity—the landscape burnt-over by the indifferent cold. Maybe you have to wonder, as you wander out under the distant stars, what it would mean to live in a universe that cared.

Or maybe, before you see, you have to step off the curb of a city street and splash into the slush of a pothole. Maybe you have to trudge up some alley, slipping with each step on the unshoveled snow, stained and crushed to patterned ice by the delivery trucks. You know that strangely sweet and sickly smell of the exhaust from diesel engines on a cold morning? Maybe you have to notice the odors of the city—the avenues insensible with crowds of harried people, hurrying about their business. Maybe you have to notice the paper cups of beggars and the pots of the red-robed Santas, ringing their Salvation Army bells while their breath steams out toward the passing traffic. Maybe you have to feel the cold heart of the city before you grasp what it would mean to live in a world of concern.

I've always thought depressed people understand Christmas best. Oh, by all psychological accounts, the season only manages to make them more depressed, more vulnerable, more prone to misery. But why wouldn't it? For the happy and the well-content, everyone out on the other end of the satisfaction spectrum, Christmas may not matter much: just a dollop, a drizzle of sweet frosting, on the wonders of winter. For the disheartened, Christmas looms much larger: the inverse of all they lack. Christmas appears as what it is—an image of optimism and hope. A picture of a cosmos capable of love.

My neighbor was decorating his house. Well before Thanksgiving, I saw him up on the rooftop. Out on the driveway, spilling from the boxes he had hauled from the garage, were plastic candy canes and an inflatable sleigh. A crèche, too, but mostly the secularized and faintly commercial elements of the holiday season: Frosty the Snowman. Illuminated icicles to hang from the eaves. Elves you knew were from the North Pole because they came with a mailbox that read *Santa's Workshop, North Pole*.

We chatted a little, once he had come down the ladder, gone back up to get the staple gun he'd forgotten, then come back down again. I joked with him about how mid-November seemed a little early. I hadn't even gotten my Thanksgiving turkey, but here he was decorating for Christmas. And he admitted the season had spilled its banks, pouring out of Advent. The grocery store had its first Christmas items for sale the week before Halloween. Still, he told me, he just enjoyed getting ready for the holiday too much to let it wait. And back he went to work, illuminating his house with all the paraphernalia of the season.

The curious thing is that without Christmas there might not be lights for him to put up. Or electricity and plastic and all the strange gifts of human progress—since Christmas brought the idea of progress sprawling into birth. A new kind of optimism. A new kind of hope.

A sense of the world as moving toward a goal, a picture of humanity as changing in history, begins with the gradual absorbing into the human psyche of the idea that history is meaningful. And that idea spreads into the world in good part from the belief that God has entered history. At the highest metaphysical level, the divine cares about the temporal order. At the furthest reaches of being, the supernatural is concerned with the natural.

As a culture these days, we may lack a clear vision of where that progress is going or even (given the number of the fashionably pessimistic) of what makes it progress. But the key is the sense that time matters. And that came to us from Christmas. In the traditional Church calendar, Advent is a penitential season, precisely in order that Christmas would mark a difference— just as progress, optimism, and hope take their meaning from a sense of a darkness that came before.

Maybe, to get it, you have to see the snowy fields, still and lonely beneath the frozen sky. Or maybe you have to plunge into the winter city, your cold hands jammed into your pockets as the uncaring crowds stream by. Or maybe you just have to put up some decorations. But one way or another, Christmas promises that there is a light in darkness, a fire in winter. And therefore be merry. Set sorrow aside.

The Ghost of Christmas Past

It's almost impossible not to know how it opens. "Marley was dead: to begin with. There is no doubt whatever about that." Charles Dickens's *A Christmas Carol* has been filmed over forty times and dramatized for the stage in dozens of versions—the first almost immediately after the book's publication in 1843, a pirated play that Dickens spent £700 to fight before he won an uncollectable judgment against its producers (and thereby found material for the great Chancery case of *Jarndyce and Jarndyce* that lies at the center of *Bleak House,* but that's another story). "Old Marley was as dead as a door-nail," the famous first paragraph of *A Christmas Carol* ends, as everyone remembers.

But who remembers how the second paragraph runs? "Mind! I don't mean to say that I know, of my own knowledge, what there is particularly dead about a door-nail. I might have been inclined, myself, to regard a coffin-nail as the deadest piece of ironmongery in the trade. But the wisdom of our ancestors is in the simile; and my unhallowed hands shall not disturb it, or the Country's done for. You will therefore permit me to repeat, emphatically, that Marley was as dead as a door-nail."

You don't get much of that narrator's voice in the films we've all seen, over and over, every Christmas—with Alastair Sim in the 1951 version, or George C. Scott in the 1984 version, or Mr. Magoo in the 1962 cartoon, for that matter. You don't get the wordiness: "I don't mean to say that I know, of my own knowledge, what there is particularly." You don't get the facetiousness: "my unhallowed hands shall not disturb it, or the Country's done for." You don't get the hallucinogenic animation of inanimate objects. You don't get the comedy running over and under the sentimentality. You don't get the manic speed, or the almost insane energy, or the sheer delight in writing down words. You may get the story, but you don't get Dickens.

And as for that story, it is, on its face, something of a mess. Of course, we don't demand much coherence from the plot, which is in itself a revealing fact about the success of Dickens's art. His friend, unofficial agent, and biographer, John Forster, claimed that Dickens took a "secret delight" in giving "a higher form" to nursery stories, and the fairy-tale quality is one of the things the reader feels immediately in *A Christmas Carol*. You would no more complain of its creaky plot than you would demand greater structural integrity for *Rumpelstiltskin*.

But we have to admit the plot isn't what anyone would call tight. After talking to Marley's ghost until "past two" in the morning, Scrooge "went straight to bed, without undressing," only to awake to meet the Ghost of Christmas Past at midnight—two hours before he fell asleep and "clad but slightly in his slippers, dressing-gown, and nightcap."

Well, as the reformed Scrooge says on Christmas morning, "The Spirits have done it all in one night. They can do anything they like. Of course they can." One feels pedantic objecting to the illogic of ghosts, but in *A Christmas Carol* they behave more inconsistently than even ghosts deserve. Apparently nothing the poor Ghost of Christmas Yet To Come shows Scrooge comes true. Bob Cratchit won't weep, "My little, little child! . . . My little child!" at the memory of his departed son—for at the story's end, after Scrooge's reformation, we are assured that Tiny Tim "did not die."

The new Scrooge will presumably meet his own death not alone, his very bed curtains stolen from around his corpse, but surrounded by his adoring nephew Fred, Fred's wife, Fred's wife's plump sister, and even Tiny Tim, to whom he will become "a second father."

Even the Ghost of Christmas Present doesn't manage to get much right. The guests at Fred's Christmas party won't make fun of the absent Scrooge, because Scrooge will be there. The Cratchits won't have their little goose, "eked out by apple-sauce and mashed potatoes." They'll have instead the enormous "prize turkey" Scrooge has sent: "He never could have stood

upon his legs, that bird. He would have snapped 'em short off in a minute, like sticks of sealing-wax." John Sutherland, the marvelous solver of minor literary problems in such books as *Was Heathcliff a Murderer?* and *Who Betrays Elizabeth Bennett?*, has a funny little note about the problems the family faced roasting that turkey. No wonder Bob Cratchit was a "full eighteen minutes and a half" late to work the next morning. The monstrous thing wouldn't have been fully cooked until almost midnight. And didn't the Cratchits wonder where their meal had come from? For that matter, what is the poultry shop doing "half open" at six on Christmas morning—and why hasn't the poulterer already sold his prize bird, which, intended for a Christmas feast, is going to go bad in short order?

Meanwhile, the characters are as unconvincing as the plot. The critic Edmund Wilson once suggested that the solution to the main figure's psychology lies in recognizing that Scrooge is a deeply divided man who will shortly revert to his miserliness. But even to speak of "Scrooge's psychology" seems to miss the point, like demanding to see character development in Little Red Riding Hood and the Big Bad Wolf.

And yet, neither is Scrooge simply a placeholder for a fairy tale's moral of conversion. He was probably intended to be that, but Dickens could not leave him alone. Scrooge ends up with far too much energy, taking far too much joy in being joyless. "If I could work my will . . . every idiot who goes about with 'Merry Christmas' on his lips, should be boiled with his own pudding, and buried with a stake of holly through his heart." "You may be an undigested bit of beef, a blot of mustard, a crumb of cheese, a fragment of an underdone potato," he says to Marley's ghost. "There's more of gravy than of grave about you, whatever you are!" He's Ralph Nickleby and Arthur Gride, the businessmen villains of *Nicholas Nickleby*, ratcheted up too much to be a mere marker of villainy—just as, after his conversion, he's *Nicholas Nickleby*'s Cheeryble brothers cranked up in absolutely insane glee: "Shaving was not an easy task, for his hand continued to shake very much; and shaving requires attention, even when you don't dance while you are at it."

It isn't just Scrooge that Dickens can't leave alone. He can't leave anything alone—which is exactly what ends up making *A Christmas Carol* a triumph: the energy, the madness, the darting from thing to thing, the extravagance invested in every moment. George Orwell spotted this in

126

Dickens. His fiction contains thousands of named characters, and every single one of them has more put in him than necessary. Even the unnamed characters can't help becoming Dickensian. While Scrooge and the Ghost of Christmas Past watch old Fezziwig's party, "In came the cook, with her brother's particular friend, the milkman. In came the boy from over the way, who was suspected of not having board enough from his master, trying to hide himself behind the girl from next door but one."

Why do we have to know all this? Dickens is like some mad magician, incapable of *not* transforming each thing that happens to catch his eye. In the obituary he wrote for the *Times* when Dickens died, Anthony Trollope seemed almost to complain about how unfair it was: Every other novelist has to bend his fiction to match reality, while reality bent itself to match Dickens; by the time he was done creating the fictional Oliver Twist, the fictional Sam Weller, or the fictional Scrooge, real orphans, bootboys, and misers had turned themselves into Dickensian characters.

The various theories that dominated twentieth-century criticism never quite figured out what to do with Dickens. The literary Edwardians wanted to detest him for what they thought of as his sentimentality, his indulgence of the grotesque, and his female characters desexualized into "legless angels"—and also for his Victorian energy, so alien to their own ironic lethargy. There were moments during the century when Freudian interpretation seemed to grant some real insights into literature (although, as Harold Bloom put it, one always felt that Shakespeare was a better reader of Freud than Freud was of Shakespeare). But one of the reasons Freudianism failed as a theory of literary interpretation is that it could never get its arms around Dickens. He didn't seem to have any psychology at all in his books—just psychological truth.

Social criticism, in its turn, tried to claim Dickens as merely the unsystematic brother of Marx and Engels, and *A Christmas Carol* as simply the popular version of *The Condition of the Working Classes in England in 1844.* More sensible critics did little better, consistently preferring to think about authors like William Makepeace Thackeray and George Eliot instead. Louis Cazamian found little in Dickens besides a *philosophie de Noël.* Orwell knew in his bones that Dickens was an author "worth fighting for," and yet he finally had to argue against Scrooge's conversion, on the grounds that Dickens never grasped the social (as opposed to the personal) structure of evil. F.R. and Q.D. Leavis painted themselves into such a corner that they ended up insisting *Hard Times* was Dickens's most important work. Even critics as good as Edmund Wilson and Lionel Trilling didn't really succeed: They were too honest to deny that Dickens was the great writer of his age, but they preferred to read authors on whom they could actually use their critical gifts.

Curiously, postmodernism managed better, not in its multicultural aspect of race, class, and gender, but in its fascination with language—for one of the things that makes Dickens run is language. Think of the names in his fiction: Scrooge and Jarndyce and Betsy Trotwood and Oliver Twist. And think of his propensity for describing inanimate objects with the adjectives of life. In the Cratchits' kitchen, the "potatoes, bubbling up, knocked loudly at the saucepan-lid to be let out and peeled." Scrooge has "a gloomy suite of rooms, in a lowering pile of building up a yard, where it had so little business to be, that one could scarcely help fancying it must have run there when it was a young house, playing at hide-and-seek with other houses, and have forgotten the way out again."

The most Dickensian moment early in *A Christmas Carol* comes when Scrooge arrives home in the evening to see Marley's face in his door-knocker: "He did pause, with a moment's irresolution, before he shut the door; and he did look cautiously behind it first, as if he half expected to be terrified with the sight of Marley's pigtail sticking out into the hall." English literature has had perhaps a dozen authors who could or would have done the door-knocker. Only Dickens is capable of the pigtail.

At the appearance of the Ghost of Christmas Present, Dickens squanders five hundred words (out of twenty-eight thousand in the story as a whole) describing the shops of a fruiter and a grocer:

> There were great, round, pot-bellied baskets of chestnuts, shaped like the waistcoats of jolly old gentlemen, lolling at the doors, and tumbling out into the street in their apoplectic opulence. There were ruddy, brown-faced, broad-girthed Spanish Onions, shining in the fatness of their growth like Spanish Friars, and winking from their shelves in wanton slyness at the girls as they went by, and glanced demurely at the hung-up mistletoe. There were . . . Norfolk Biffins, squab and swarthy, setting off the yellow of the oranges and lemons, and, in the great compactness of their juicy persons, urgently entreating and beseeching to be carried home in paper bags and eaten after dinner.

That phrase "the great compactness of their juicy persons" could be imitated if one tried. Most parodies of Dickens get no further than the Dickensian sentimentality and *philosophie de Noël.* But it was this sort of odd, wordy construction that James Joyce seized upon when he reached Dickens in his historical parodies of English prose in the maternity chapter of *Ulysses.* And the truth is that Dickens's language could be peculiar; this is the man who gave English the phrase "our mutual friend," for example, when what he meant was a shared or common friend.

What can't be imitated, however, is the energy. The Edwardians were right about Dickens's Victorianism—except that he was a hyper-Victorian, with all the virtues and vices of his age raised to something like the platonic ideal by the enormous power of his stamina. The biographer

Edgar Johnson seems mistaken when he says that Christmas has for Dickens only "the very smallest connection with Christian theology or dogma." There's plenty of Christianity in the Christmas books, from the preface, in which Dickens claims his purpose was to write "a whimsical kind of masque" that might "awaken some loving and forbearing thoughts, never out of season in a Christian land," to the most sentimental moment in *A Christmas Carol,* in which Tiny Tim "hoped the people saw him in the church, because he was a cripple, and it might be pleasant to them to remember upon Christmas Day, who made lame beggars walk, and blind men see."

But Johnson is at least correct that the secularizing impulse has begun its implacable work. Even G.K. Chesterton, normally Dickens's most consistent defender, complained that Dickens, faced with the single event around which the world has developed the most mythology, decided to invent his own Christmas mythology. But that's because traditional Christmas images actually involve the Christ who will become the Savior with his death and resurrection, and Dickens always wanted to avoid the hard cosmological edges of Christian theology. To read *The Life of Our Lord* that Dickens wrote for his own children is to think the key moment in Christian history is Christmas, not Easter, and the key teaching of Jesus is "Suffer little children, and forbid them not to come unto me: for of such is the kingdom of heaven." This is a serious diminishment of what St. Paul knew was the scandal of Christianity, but it is very Victorian—a reflection of all that was advanced, generous, liberal, high-minded, and doomed in the Gladstonian vision of a modern Christian state. "English flatheads" and "little moralistic females *à la* George Eliot," Nietzsche called them, who thought they could preserve Christian morality without much Christian theology.

In the months before *A Christmas Carol* was written in 1843, the serial publication of *Martin Chuzzlewit* had not been going well, the first of Dickens's full novels to enjoy less than universal acclaim. His sending of his characters Martin Chuzzlewit and Mark Tapley off to America helped, and, as he later noted, the book gradually "forced itself up in people's opinion." But Dickens lived on his popularity; he needed esteem, and the tepid response to *Martin Chuzzlewit* brought home to him just how tired he was. He was supporting a huge household beyond his income, he had to act as his own promoter and copyright protector, and he had written six major novels in seven years. "It is impossible to go on working the brain to that extent for ever," he told Forster. "The very spirit of the thing, in doing it, leaves a horrible despondency behind."

So he decided, in cold, commercial calculation, that he would write a Christmas story and make the £1,000 he needed to take his family away to Italy for a long vacation. Of course, being Dickens, he couldn't leave it alone. He began *A Christmas Carol* early in October and completed it before the end of November—while, as he described it, he "wept and laughed, and wept again, and excited himself in a most extraordinary manner in the composition; and thinking whereof he walked about the black streets of London fifteen and twenty miles many a night when all sober folk had gone to bed." Demanding to oversee every aspect of publication, he forced upon his publisher expensive plates and bindings, and although the book's first printing sold out in a single day, the initial quarter's profits brought him less than a third of the money for which he had hoped.

That, too, was Dickens. As prolific and well-paid a major author as there has ever been, he was always living not on what he had done but on money received for the promise of what he would do next. When *A Christmas Carol* was finished, he and Forster "broke out" like madmen, with "such dinings, such dancings, such conjurings, such blind-man's-bluffings, such theatre-goings, such kissings-out of old years and kissings-in of new ones [as] never took place in these parts before. . . . And if you could have seen me at the children's party at Macready's the other night . . . "

Jane Carlyle did see him at that party for the actor William Charles Macready's children. She hadn't slept well for weeks—hadn't slept at all the night before—and she was quarreling again with her husband, Thomas Carlyle. But once there, she found herself, like everyone else, caught up in the Dickensian world. "Dickens and Forster, above all, exerted themselves till the perspiration was pouring down and they seemed *drunk* with their efforts," she described it in a letter.

> Only think of that excellent Dickens playing the *conjuror* for one whole hour—the *best* conjuror I ever saw. . . . Then the dancing, . . . the gigantic Thackeray &c &c all capering like *Maenades*!! . . . *After supper* when we were all madder than ever with the pulling of crackers, the drinking of champagne, and the making of speeches; a universal country dance was proposed—and Forster *seizing me round the waist* whirled me into the thick of it, and *made* me dance!! like a person in the treadmill who must move forward or be crushed to death. Once I cried out, "Oh for the love of Heaven let me go! you are going to dash my brains out against the folding doors!" "Your *brains*!!" he answered, "who cares about their brains *here*? *Let them go*!"

The party rose "to something not unlike the *rape of the Sabines*!" and then Dickens carried Forster and Thackeray off to his house "'*to finish the night there*' and a *royal* night they would have of it I fancy!" But Jane Carlyle went home and slept—and slept and slept, her first healthy sleep in what felt to her like years.

There's some deep reflection in that scene, an image for the age: The mad Victorian extrovert Charles Dickens, his most popular story just finished, gathering up everyone around him and infusing them like puppets with his own Christmas energy. And in it, the mad Victorian introvert Jane Carlyle at last finding peace.

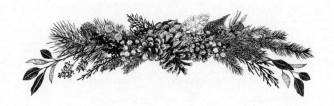

The Poetry of Christmas

"Then pealed the bells more loud and deep: / 'God is not dead, nor doth He sleep,'" Henry Wadsworth Longfellow proclaims in the tremendous final verse of his 1865 Civil War poem "Christmas Bells." We tend to forget how significant a figure Longfellow seemed in the nineteenth century—how significant poetry itself seemed, for that matter.

By the 1880s, the poem was a standard in church hymnals and parlor songbooks under the title "I Heard the Bells on Christmas Day," with a melody by the organist John Baptiste Calkin:

> *I heard the bells on Christmas Day*
> *Their old, familiar carols play,*
> *And wild and sweet*
> *The words repeat*
> *Of peace on earth, good-will to men!*

> *And thought how, as the day had come,*
> *The belfries of all Christendom*
> *Had rolled along*
> *The unbroken song*
> *Of peace on earth, good-will to men!*

Even back in Longfellow's era, something in the season prevented us from leaving Christmas poems alone. To this day we feel compelled to turn them into carols, to belt them out as lyrics, and not all poetry survives the experience. It's close to impossible not to know Clement Clarke Moore's ridiculously catchy light-verse poem from 1823, "A Visit from St. Nicholas." It has a claim to be the most popular American poem ever published, but most Americans these days probably learn it first as a song:

> *'Twas the night before Christmas, when all through the house*
> *Not a creature was stirring, not even a mouse;*
> *The stockings were hung by the chimney with care,*
> *In hopes that St. Nicholas soon would be there;*
> *The children were nestled all snug in their beds;*
> *While visions of sugar-plums danced in their heads.*

In truth, it's a pretty good song—as is the carol "In the Bleak Midwinter," which began as an 1872 poem by Christina Rossetti. When it comes to music, "I Heard the Bells on Christmas Day" wasn't as lucky. Calkin's melody is far from perfect, and while a 1956 setting by the composer Johnny Marks is better, it's not enough to make the song as popular as "Twelve Days of Christmas" or "Deck the Halls."

Still, Longfellow's lines remain something like a primer, a blueprint, for modern Christmas poetry. He ends each verse with the refrain "peace on earth, good-will to men"—a technique of repetition found in many Christmas poems, from the repeated "pale-green, fairy mistletoe" in Walter de la Mare's "Mistletoe" to the echoing "every stone shall cry" in Richard Wilbur's "A Christmas Hymn."

Bells, too, are a constant Christmas theme, from John Betjeman's "The bells of waiting Advent ring" to Alfred Tennyson's "Ring out, wild bells":

> *Ring out the old, ring in the new,*
> *Ring, happy bells, across the snow:*
> *The year is going, let him go;*
> *Ring out the false, ring in the true.*
>
> *Ring out the grief that saps the mind*
> *For those that here we see no more;*
> *Ring out the feud of rich and poor,*
> *Ring in redress to all mankind.*

But most of all, what Longfellow helped to establish was nostalgia as a defining theme of modern Christmas verses. Packed into his phrase "the old, familiar carols" is all the wistfulness—the sense of a purer feeling for Christmas in childhood—the nineteenth century bequeathed to us.

There had been Christmas poetry before the Victorians, of course, but it tended to be theological and biblical rather than sentimental. "Love is the fire," wrote Robert Southwell in his powerful Christmas poem "The Burning Babe." A Jesuit martyr hanged by Queen Elizabeth's priest-hunters in 1595, Southwell imagines the newborn Christ purifying the world like a blacksmith's fire:

> *"The metal in this furnace wrought are men's defiled souls,*
> *For which, as now on fire I am to work them to their good,*
> *So will I melt into a bath to wash them in my blood."*
> *With this he vanish'd out of sight and swiftly shrunk away,*
> *And straight I called unto mind that it was Christmas day.*

So, too, John Milton pictures the cosmic consequences of the child's birth in his 1629 "On the Morning of Christ's Nativity," writing that Jesus "our deadly forfeit should release, / And with his Father work us a perpetual peace."

By the end of the nineteenth century, however, childhood nostalgia had so flooded Christmas verses that, in the worst of them, theology and the Bible were drowned in sickly sweet syrup. Still, the best remain classics. Thomas Hardy's 1915 poem "The Oxen," for example, has a pitch-perfect ending that just escapes sentimentality:

> *If someone said on Christmas Eve,*
> *"Come; see the oxen kneel,*
> *In the lonely barton by yonder coomb*
> *Our childhood used to know,"*
> *I should go with him in the gloom,*
> *Hoping it might be so.*

The theme continued through the twentieth century and beyond. In "[little tree]," E.E. Cummings pictures himself as a child by a "silent Christmas tree": "my little sister and i will take hands / and looking up at our beautiful tree / we'll dance and sing." In "Tinsel, Frankincense, and Fir," Dana Gioia is overwhelmed by recollections of his mother as he unpacks old Christmas ornaments. Each flap of an "Advent Calendar," writes Gjertrud Schnackenberg, "is childhood's shrunken door."

Longfellow began his Christmas poem after his son was injured fighting against the Confederates, and he describes how Christian hope struggles to celebrate the Prince of Peace during a time of war: "Then from each black, accursed mouth / The cannon thundered in the South." That contrast, that ironhearted irony, threads through any number of modern Christmas poems. A bitter 1960s poem by Charles Causley, for example, looks at human interaction after the holidays, on "The Thirteenth Day of Christmas," and sees only a world of war where "the greasy guns bellow."

What Longfellow also understood, however, is that Christmas will not be defined by our failures to apply its lessons and carols. We celebrate the promise of redemption, he thought, because we have need of that redemption. And so he ends "Christmas Bells" as a Christmas poem ought to end—with an embrace of the promise of the newborn child: "The Wrong shall fail, / The Right prevail," he prays, "With peace on earth, good-will to men."

The End of Advent

What happens when Christmas absorbs the conditions for its own meaning? When the huge, ungainly thing grows so big that it eats up even its Christianity? For Christmas has, over the past century, devoured Advent, gobbling it up with the turkey giblets and the goblets of seasonal ale. Yes, yes, I know: Every secularized holiday tends to lose, in public contexts, the meaning it holds in the religious calendar. Across the nation, even in some of the churches, Easter has hopped across Lent, Halloween has frightened away All Saints, and New Year's has swallowed up Epiphany.

Still, the disappearance of Advent in our common understanding is a difficulty—for it's injured even the secular Christmas season: opening a hole, from Thanksgiving on, that can be filled only with fiercer, madder, and wilder attempts to anticipate Christmas. More Christmas trees. More Christmas lights. More tinsel, more tassels, more glitter, more glee—until the glut of candies and carols, ornaments and trimmings, has left almost nothing for Christmas Day. For much of America—even for me, out here in the Black Hills of South Dakota—Christmas itself arrives as an afterthought: not the fulfillment, but only the end, of the long yule season that has burned without stop since the stores began their Christmas sales.

It's true that in the liturgical calendar, the season points ahead to Christmas. Advent genuinely proclaims an *advent*—a time before, a looking forward—and it lacks meaning without Christmas. But maybe Christmas, in turn, lacks meaning without the penitential season of Advent to go before it. The daily Bible readings in the churches during Advent are filled with visions of things yet to be—a constant barrage of the future tense. Think of Isaiah's *And it shall come to pass . . . And there shall come forth . . .* A longing pervades the Old Testament selections read in the weeks before

Christmas—an anxious, almost sorrowful litany of hope only in what has not yet come. Zephaniah. Judges. Malachi. Numbers. *I shall see him, but not now: I shall behold him, but not nigh: There shall come a star out of Jacob, and a scepter shall rise out of Israel.*

At its root, Advent is a discipline: a way of forming anticipation and channeling it toward its goal. There's a flicker of rose on the third Sunday— *Gaudete!*, the Latin of that day's Mass begins: *Rejoice!*—but then it's back to the dark purple that is the sign of the season in liturgical churches. And what those somber vestments symbolize is the atonement and promise of reform we make during Advent. Nothing we do can earn us the gift of Christmas, any more than Lent wins us Easter. But a season of contrition and sacrifice prepares us to understand and feel something about just how great the gift is when at last the day itself arrives.

More than any other holiday, Christmas seems to need its setting in the church year, for without it we have a diminishment of language, a diminishment of culture, and a diminishment of imagination. The Jesse trees and the Advent calendars, St. Martin's Fast and St. Nicholas's Feast—the childless crèches, the candle wreaths, the vigil of Christmas Eve: They give a shape to the anticipation of the season. They discipline the ideas and emotions that would otherwise shake themselves to pieces, like a flywheel wobbling wilder and wilder until it finally snaps off its axle.

Maybe that's what has happened to Christmas, in the days since Dickens bestrode the season. The ideas and the emotions have all broken free and smashed their way across the fields. From Longfellow's *I heard the bells on Christmas Day / Their old, familiar carols play* to Irving Berlin's *I'm dreaming of a white Christmas / Just like the ones I used to know*, there has been, for a long time now, something oddly backward looking about Christmas lyrics—some nostalgia that insists on substituting its melancholy for the somber contrition and sorrow of Advent. In the same way, childhood memoirs have become the dominant form of Christmas writing. Often beautiful—from Dylan Thomas's *A Child's Christmas in Wales* to Lillian Smith's *Memories of a Large Christmas*—those stories nonetheless deploy their golden-hued Christmassy emotions only toward the past: a kind of contrite feeling without the structure of Advent's contrition; all the regret and sense of absence cast back to what has been and never will be again.

Meanwhile, weirdly, the forward-looking parts of Advent have also escaped the discipline of the season. In certain ways, the season has become little except anticipation—anticipation run amuck, like children so sick with expectation that the reality can never be satisfying when it finally arrives. This, too, is something broken off from the liturgical year: another group of adventual feelings without the Advent that gave them form, another set of Christmas ideas set loose to drive themselves mad.

Back in the early 1890s, William Dean Howells published a funny little fable called "Christmas Every Day." Once upon a time, the story begins, "there was a little girl who liked Christmas so much that she wanted it to be Christmas every day in the year." What's more, she found a fairy to grant her wish, and she was delighted when Christmas came again on December 26, and December 27, and December 28.

Of course, "after it had gone on about three or four months, the little girl, whenever she came into the room in the morning and saw those great ugly, lumpy stockings dangling at the fireplace, and the disgusting presents around everywhere, used to sit down and burst out crying. In six months she was perfectly exhausted, she couldn't even cry anymore." By October, "people didn't carry presents around nicely anymore. They flung them over the fence or through the window, and, instead of taking great pains to write 'For dear Papa,' or 'Mama' or 'Brother,' or 'Sister,' they used to write, 'Take it, you horrid old thing!' and then go and bang it against the front door."

These days, by the time Christmas actually rolls around, it feels as though this is very nearly what we've had: Christmas every day, at least since Thanksgiving. Often it starts even earlier. This year I started receiving the glossy catalogues of Christmas clothing and seasonal bric-a-brac in September, and there were Christmas-shopping ads on the highway billboards before Halloween. The anticipatory elements reach a crescendo by early December, and their constant scream makes the sudden quiet of Christmas Day almost a relief from the Christmas season.

I don't remember quite this much opposition, the battle between Christmas and the Christmas season, when I was young. When I was little (ah, the nostalgia of the childhood memoir), I always felt that the days right before Christmas were a time somehow out of time. Christmas Eve, especially, and the arrival of Christmas itself at midnight: the hours moved in ways different from their passage in ordinary time, and the sense of impending completion was like a flavor to the air I breathed.

I've noticed in recent years, however, that this feeling comes over me more rarely than it used to, and for shorter bits of time. I have to pursue the sense of wonder, the taste in the air, and cling to it self-consciously. Even for me, the endless roar of untethered Christmas anticipation is close to drowning out the disciplined anticipation of Advent. And when Christmas itself arrives, it has begun to seem a day not all that different from any other. Oh, yes, church and home to a big dinner. Presents for the children. A set of decorations. But nothing special, really.

This is what Advent, rightly kept, would halt—the thing, in fact, Advent is designed to prevent. Through all the preparatory readings, through all the genealogical Jesse trees, the somber candles on the wreaths, the vigils, and the hymns, Advent keeps Christmas on Christmas Day: a fulfillment, a perfection and completion, of what had gone before. *I shall see him, but not now: I shall behold him, but not nigh.*

The Second Day of Christmas

It's turtle doves today. The two of them we're supposed to receive on the 26th of December, the second day of Christmas. The turtle dove—as you know, of course—is the *Streptopelia turtur*: a member of the family Columbidae, a migratory species native to Europe and North Africa with a southern Palearctic migratory range. Smaller and slighter than their non-turtley cousins, turtle doves may be recognized by their brown color and the striped patch on the side of their necks.

And so "the voice of the turtle is heard in our land," the King James Version of Song of Songs reports, either because turtles were especially noisy in the days of King Solomon or because the English in the seventeenth century didn't know many turtles personally and thought the creatures wouldn't mind sharing their name with a bunch of doves.

Actually, a little research will show that the words are unrelated: *turtle* for turtle doves is a Middle English imitation of the turturing sound the birds make, while *turtle* for turtles comes from the Latin *tortuca* for tortoise, via the French *tortue*. And, anyway, it was the doves we are supposed to get today, for the second day of Christmas, according to the song, not the ectothermic *Testudines* reptiles.

And that's the point I was trying to make, before the Linnaean system of biological classification and the weirdness of English words distracted me. The twelve days of Christmas aren't the run-up to Christmas, culminating in the smash-up of twelve drummers drumming on Christmas Day. They are the run of days in the season afterward, as Christmas reaches out toward the coming year.

This is what we've gotten wrong with the way we tend to do Christmas. The days before the holy day, the weeks marked with Advent candles, were intended to be penitential—a season of reflection and amends, with the celebration starting mostly on the actual day of Christ's birth. Advent was intended to make us look forward to the parties, but we've turned the pre-Christmas days into the celebration itself. And what, then, are we supposed to do in the time right after Christmas? What are we supposed to do for the next twelve nights?

In the complexities of the Church calendar, Christmas Day is the end of the four weeks of Advent and the first of the days of Christmas, which run till January fifth. And, as Shakespeare knew, that last Christmas evening is called Twelfth Night: the night before Epiphany and traditionally a time for skits and celebrations, with a Lord of Misrule appointed to lead the festivities.

The Christmas season gives us the Feast of St. Stephen (Boxing Day in England, Wren Day in Ireland, and December 26 in the rest of the world). And then the feast of the Holy Innocents, the children slaughtered by King Herod. And then the feast of the Holy Family; Hogmanay, the feast of St. Sylvester; the Solemnity of Mary, the feast of the Holy Name, and all the rest.

What a muddle it can seem. Even in the Church calendar, the run from the first day of Christmas through to Epiphany and on to Candlemas has no clarity of narrative, no firmness of organization, and no sharpness of lesson—except, perhaps, in the sheer messiness of it all. Despite all the advertisements and canned carols that begin even before Thanksgiving, Advent is structured as a clean and penitential time. Christmas itself is the chaos.

But Christmas isn't supposed to be tidy, and that's rather the message that the Church conveys in the season. Christmas is supposed to radiate on through the next days, with the turtle doves and all the progressively more absurd and extravagant gifts named in the song. Christmas is one of those medieval festivals, which were always wild and unruly things—a theological center to it all, but wrapped around that center are layers and layers of mad celebrations, wild decorations, and boisterous song.

Layers and layers of joy, in other words. The Christmas season isn't the calm of Christmas Eve and the silence of the Holy Night and all the rest of the whispered anticipations of Advent. Christmas is when the real thing has actually arrived—Christ, born in the flesh—and the time has come to celebrate.

In the way we celebrate Christmas these days, we have substituted a modern festival for a medieval one. There's no single cause. The Modern Age was born from disparate elements—the scientific revolution, capitalism, the rise of democracy and all the rest—somehow joining to push us out of the Middle Ages. And so with modern Christmas. A secularizing impulse tried to save the festivities by giving us nonreligious tropes that could slip past the wall of church-state relations: Santa and Rudolph. Trees without Christian decorations. Candy canes. Cards that say "happy holidays." School concerts that promise "winter carols." Frosty the Snowman, may God have mercy on us all.

From the 1870s on, commercialization added its own power, shoving the season forward in a frenzy of purchased-gift-giving and "after Christmas" sales. The modern suspicion of the medieval as unscientific and unenlightened did its usual disenchanting of the old festivals, aided by Western Christianity's modern stripping of the layered accretions the Middle Ages had built up.

Fortunately, Christmas is enormous enough, extreme enough, insurmountable enough, that it can survive even its transformation into a modern holiday. A blaze of light and warmth in the cold of winter, matching its joyous psychology with a preference for bright colors and silly inflatable reindeer. An incarnation in the literal sense: the Word made flesh. A sound of bells and carols in the silent night.

Still, Christmas would be even better if we remembered that the celebration naturally extends after Christmas, not before. We could use a return of the skits and the old tradition of Christmas ghost stories. We could do with the community of the Christmas markets in the town square, lasting through to Epiphany on January 6—or even Candlemas on February 2. We could benefit from reviving the dance of Twelfth Night, overseen by a Lord of Misrule. We could stand a little more medievalism in our lives. Just in time for Christmas.

Nearly everyone knows how to do Christmas Day. In our house, over the years, we folded together some of my wife's parent's traditions with some of my own parent's traditions, seasoned by things that caught our eye or taste buds: a Swedish dried-fruit soup for Christmas Eve and those round Danish pancakes called aebleskivers for Christmas morning. (Lots of Scandinavians, out in the Dakotas where I grew up.) A roast goose, sage stuffing, cranberries, and all the other trimmings for Christmas dinner. A tree with silver sleigh bells and glass ornaments, a mantel with stockings and a crèche. All the panoply of wreathes and bows and lights and bells.

But it's in the days after Christmas that we see Christmas unfold—the days of eggnog and leftovers. The jigsaw puzzles spread out on the folding table. The games and the skits. The annual ghost stories. The visits with the neighbors. The cold and the dry snow that crunches underneath your boots. It's not coherent, and it's not neat, anymore than that silly partridge in the pear tree makes much sense. But it is a sign of the Christmas truth about the great, mad joy that God brought into the world. And so I'll take it— along with the two turtle doves I'm owed the next day.

The Mind of the Magi

How much do we trust the mind? How much *should* we—when thoughts lead on to thoughts, conjectures build atop conjectures, hypotheses extend upon hypotheses until it all seems just . . . too . . . much, a daydream from which we shake ourselves awake?

The crèches that come out at Christmas, crowding the side table in the living room or overflowing on the mantel, usually surround the Holy Family with animals and angels gazing at the child in the manger. Plus the shepherds, of course, and the Wise Men.

Of them all, the Wise Men—the Magi, the Three Kings—may be the oddest. From Mary and Joseph to the shepherds and the kneeling animals, a crèche shows us mostly figures of faith. But the Magi seem to represent something else. They are symbols and icons not of simple faith but of trust in the power of the mind.

Think of it this way. The rural shepherds came down from the hills because the angels appeared and told them of the Savior's birth. The animals were all on their knees, moved by the visible sight of the divine. But the Magi had to have set out long before, in order to arrive in time. They had to read the stars, the signs ofconjectures build atop conjectures, hypotheses extend upon hypotheses until it all seems just . . . too . . . much, a daydream from which we shake ourselves awake?

The crèches that come out at Christmas, crowding the side table in the living room or overflowin the age and the deep meanings of the universe— and then act on what they thought they had discerned. These were city dwellers and learned people, and when a great star appeared in the sky, they followed their intellectual curiosity and journeyed off to discover where it led. They brought gifts, because they wanted to honor the newborn king

for whom they were searching. More to the point, they brought gifts because they imagined they might actually find him.

All of which is to say, they had the intelligence to examine honestly
the clues the world offered them. They had the wisdom to seek the truth
for its own sake, whatever it might prove to be. These are believers in the
mind, in other words, who undertook a great expedition because they
trusted their thoughts, conjectures, and hypotheses—and refused to shake
themselves back into the small thoughts of ordinary life.

"A cold coming they had of it, the worst time of the year to take a
long journey. The ways deep, the weather sharp, the days short, the sun
farthest off: in *solsitio brumali*, the very dead of winter." Or so Lancelot
Andrewes preached, to King James I on Christmas Day 1622, about the
Journey of the Magi to see the newborn Christ.

The Magi occupy such an odd layer of the vast panoply of Christmas
legends that wrap the holiday like festive paper. Only the Gospel of St.
Matthew mentions them in the Bible, and even Matthew's Nativity story
leaves them unnamed. Gold, frankincense, and myrrh, the Gospel reports
they brought as gifts and homage, and from the numbering of three gifts
there emerged in early Christianity the legend that there were three of
them: the Three Kings, the three Wise Men.

Even the day of their arrival is uncertain. Though crèches often show
them gathered at the manger, Matthew has the Magi finding Mary and
Jesus sometime later in a house (*oikos*, in the Greek of the Gospel). That
visit may have come as much as two years later (since after speaking with
the Magi, Herod orders the death of all boys up to two years old, in the
Massacre of the Innocents), or it may have come as soon as two weeks
after his birth—on Epiphany, January 6, the Magi's traditional feast day
in the Western church.

Tradition has granted them the title of kings, probably after Psalm
72:11: *Yea, all kings shall fall down before him.* And tradition has given
them names, together with origins and ages of symbolic value, represent-
ing the known lands of the East and the three stages of adult life. Caspar,
a sixty-year-old man from Asia Minor or Persia, offers gold. Melchior, a
forty-year-old man from Arabia or India, comes with frankincense. And
Balthazar, a twenty-year-old man from Ethiopia or Babylon, brings
myrrh.

It's a swirl of uncertainty, with the spread of Christianity prompting different nations to identify themselves as home to the births or the deaths of the Magi—tradition squabbling with tradition about nearly every detail. Still, the initial moment in Matthew is clear: *In the days of Herod the king, behold, there came wise men from the east to Jerusalem, saying, "Where is he that is born King of the Jews? For we have seen his star in the east, and are come to worship him."*

Herod had reason to be worried. His rule as a client of the Romans was unstable. Judea was a powder-keg of religious anger, political unrest, and apocalyptic feeling. Then suddenly these distinguished scholars arrive—out of the east, out of the blue—and demand to know where they can find the new-born king, Herod's replacement, whose appearance they have read in the stars.

Interestingly, it is Herod who points them to Bethlehem, when his own scholars tell him that the prophet Micah has named the small town as the birthplace of the coming king—*a ruler in Israel; whose goings forth have been from of old, from everlasting* (Micah 5:2). And so to Bethlehem they came, following their star, to find the infant Jesus, bow before him, and give their gifts to his mother. *And being warned of God in a dream that they should not return to Herod, they departed into their own country another way.*

In his 1927 poem "The Journey of the Magi," T.S. Eliot begins with *a cold coming we had of it*, in lines adapted from Lancelot Andrewes's 1622 sermon. Eliot builds from there a dramatic monologue of an old man remembering a tedious journey he had made years before. Along the way, the man and his Magi companions saw signs and symbols of the new age that Christ has ushered in, from the Crucifixion (*three trees on the low sky*) to the Apocalypse (*an old white horse galloped away in the meadow*). But what strikes him most, even years later, is not the birth of the child and the beginning of a new world, but the death of the old order that must result from it all:

> . . . *were we led all that way for*
> *Birth or Death? There was a Birth, certainly,*
> *We had evidence and no doubt. I had seen birth and death,*
> *But had thought they were different; this Birth was*
> *Hard and bitter agony for us, like Death, our death.*
> *We returned to our places, these Kingdoms,*
> *But no longer at ease here, in the old dispensation,*
> *With an alien people clutching their gods.*
> *I should be glad of another death.*

Eliot's "Journey of the Magi" remains a powerful way to think about the Three Kings of Orient. In every gain there must be some loss, as the old gives way to the new. The unnamed Wise Man who narrates the poem proves wise enough to see the changing of the times; that is why he undertook the journey to Bethlehem and why, he says, he would do it again if he had to. But he also finds himself lost in the new day. His learning allowed him to perceive the change that Christ brought; that same learning trapped him in the old day, dying away.

I wonder, though, if this is the only way to understand the Magi. In a curious passage in the *Confessions*, St. Augustine suggests that philosophers could, at their best, foresee many things that Christianity would later reveal as true. The Platonists could observe, at least in effect, that "In the beginning was the Word, and the Word was with God, and the Word was God." They could work their minds in metaphysics, in other words, and discover deep ideas—conjectures, hypotheses—about the structure of the universe. What they couldn't discover, by philosophy alone, was the additional part: that "the Word was made flesh, and dwelt among us."

For most philosophers, it would be easy enough not to bother looking for the real instantiation of their abstract ideas. They could just shake themselves awake—returning to everyday thoughts and abandoning the trust of philosophy that might have kept them going. Typical Christmastide sermons preach on the simple faith of the shepherds who were told of the great incarnation, believed it, and came down from the hills to honor the child. Yet we shouldn't scorn the Magi's complex, tenuous work of the mind. These are the saints of the intellect. They grasped some small part of the universe's need for a savior, the philosophical signs of a new age, and they set out on a long, hard journey to find the actuality of the possibilities they discerned.

A cold coming they had of it, in truth, for the conjectures of the mind are chillier than the warmth of the shepherds' simple faith. But the Magi's trust that creation is intelligible—their certainty that the star they followed must mean something—kept them on their path until they, too, knelt before the Word made flesh.

Christmas and the Boy Reader

There were always books for Christmas. Mounds of them: flurries of paperbacks, drifts of presentation copies inscribed in the unreadably copperplate hand of maiden great aunts, avalanches of books on chess, and manuals of do-it-yourself chemistry experiments *using household items!* And teach-yourself sleight-of-hand magic guides, and the not all-that-gratefully-received Latin to English—*and English to Latin!*—dictionary. The already-too-childish children's chapter books, from distant acquaintances of our parents. The popular Victorian and Edwardian fiction, adult stories that had somehow moved down the reader's scale to be thought of as proper for young readers, marketed to harried uncles seeking something in last-minute bookstores: *The Adventures of Sherlock Holmes*, *Around the World in Eighty Days*, *The Prisoner of Zenda*, *The Scarlet Pimpernel*.

We never got Hardy Boys or Nancy Drew books. But I remember other series: Tom Swift, the Bobbsey Twins, the Rover Boys, the Wizard of Oz books, although mostly as stray and dusty copies on bookshelves in the childhood bedrooms of aunts and uncles, long since moved away from my grandmother's house. The standard girls' books of their era, too: *Pollyanna*, *Anne of Green Gables*, *Little Women*, *Rebecca of Sunnybrook Farm*, *A Little Princess*. Nothing I would have chosen, but there they were, on the old shelves, demanding to be read by a child stretched out on the faded ripcord bedspreads of a generation past.

Not that my own preferences were much better. *The Mad Scientists' Club*, for example. I ached for the book when I saw it in one of those Scholastic Books catalogues they used to hand out in school, and I couldn't understand why my mother wouldn't let me place an order, till the paperback she'd bought showed up in a Christmas stocking. My first vague inklings of sexuality came from Robert E. Howard's Conan the Barbarian books—but, then, my first creeping sense of a malevolent supernatural, like a gateway drug for H.P. Lovecraft, came from those Conan stories, too. Edgar Rice Burroughs's *Tarzan of the Apes*, Arthur Conan Doyle's *The Lost World*: a dive into the genre of lost primitivism that began with Rudyard Kipling's Mowgli in the first *Jungle Book* and ended with a thud, for me, at Rima the Bird Girl in William Henry Hudson's *Green Mansions*—just as my love of pirates began with Robert Louis Stevenson's *Treasure Island* and Rafael Sabatini's *Captain Blood*, and closed hard a few years later when someone gave me Richard Hughes's *A High Wind in Jamaica*, about the indifference of children taken by pirates.

A mistake, in those book-strewn days, was the giving of Christmas books for Christmas. The time for the tearjerkery of Henry van Dyke's *The Other Wise Man* or Kate Douglas Wiggin's *The Birds' Christmas Carol* is in Advent's toboggan run toward Christmas. Even the better Christmas books—Dickens's *A Christmas Carol,* Dylan Thomas's *A Child's Christmas in Wales,* which my parents would read aloud—need to come before the actual arrival of Christmas. I've always had a soft spot for Jean Shepherd's *A Christmas Story* and O. Henry's perfectly sappy "The Gift of the Magi," but they're for the days when the goose is getting fat. Once the goose is cooked, so are they.

But poetry began for me with Louis Untermeyer's *Golden Treasury of Poetry,* which I still have with the Christmas inscription from my grandmother, though the binding is cracked and the pages drift out like snowflakes when I take it down from the shelf. Philosophy began with Plato's *Apology* and *Crito,* which I didn't understand but seemed adult and sad. Mysteries started with Encyclopedia Brown and quickly moved to Agatha Christie's *Murder at the Vicarage* and Rex Stout's *The Golden Spiders.* Science fiction began with *A Wrinkle in Time* and *Flowers for Algernon.*

Fantasy began as a dive into the deep end with *The Lord of the Rings* when I was ten. Theology began with the lives of the saints in a children's version of the *Golden Legend*.

Every era has its advantages and disadvantages, its benefits and curses. My time saw the collapse of shared knowledge, the decay of belief in authority, the failure of confidence in culture. But books were everywhere. We had that, at least. Icebergs of books, to cling to as we set out on the sea of adulthood. Cascades of books, like heaps of snow collapsing from branch to branch down a pine tree. Avalanches of books as their unsteady stacks gave way. And Christmas was their stormhead, their North Pole origin. New authors, new genres, new worlds, new lives to live vicariously—all unwrapped at Christmas. Each examined and weighed and felt, with one chosen to sneak upstairs and read early on Christmas afternoon, while the scent of the pine tree and the kitchen's first sautéings drifted up the stairwell.

With the triumph of eBooks and eReaders these days, you can't say that text has disappeared. If anything, the computer revolution has made written words more ubiquitous, more all-surrounding, more intrusive. But the fading of physical books seems to have brought with it a fading of a category we used to acknowledge: the boy reader.

Oh, there are still boys and still books. Still boys who read. But hard to find anymore is the culturally accepted category of the boy reader, the bright little kid who inhales books like oxygen—"reading as if for life," in Dickens's description of the young David Copperfield—and wants to know everything: living in books every life, feeling in characters every emotion. The little boy who needs to grasp the world.

This is something a little different from the books listed these days by web pages with such titles as "Books That Boys Say Are Awesome." The explicitly boyish boys' book existed, back in the day, and I remember reading a worn and rebound copy of *The Kid Who Batted 1.000* in a junior-high-school library, along with such boys-at-boarding-school stories as Owen Johnson's *The Prodigious Hickey*. Bertrand R. Brinley's *Rocket Manual for Amateurs*, for that matter: boys' books, all.

But the boys of the boy-reader type would receive a copy of, say, *Lost Horizon* (a boy's book, maybe) and then want to read *Goodbye, Mr. Chips* and *Random Harvest* and the rest of James Hilton's novels. In the 1940s, the critic Lionel Trilling looked back at the sets of books that once filled the bookshelves of the middle-class (or, at least, the middle-class strivers, who wanted their children to grow up surrounded by the accoutrements of culture). And he decried the decline of the set on those family shelves—*The Works of Dickens, The Collected Writings of Thackeray, The Complete Washington Irving*—observing that, upon discovering an author, young readers would "remain loyal to him until they had read him by the yard."

Girls could read this way, too, of course, but the culture has lost the idea of the boy reader more completely than that of the girl reader. In *Strong Opinions*, a collection of his criticism, Vladimir Nabokov shows us almost the ideal model of that boy reader, turned adult. Of G.K. Chesterton, Arthur Conan Doyle, and Joseph Conrad alike, he remarks, "A favorite between the ages of 8 and 14. Essentially a writer for very young people." Hemingway is "a writer of books for boys. Certainly better than Conrad." He says of Shakespeare that he "read complete works between 14 and 15." H.G. Wells was "my favorite writer when I was a boy. His sociological cogitations can be safely ignored, but his romances and fantasies are superb."

Few of us are Trillings or Nabokovs, of course, but they belonged in adulthood to a recognizable type, having been boy readers (in an era with an almost moral distinction, greater than my later time held, of the difference between literature culturally recognized as great and books that were merely popular or fun). And recognition of that type has clearly faded. I paid a Christmas visit to a distant neighbor's house early last December, a family with lots of kids and cousins, all of them bright. But as the parents wrapped packages while we chatted, I noticed the absence of books—the physical hard copies that had been the center of Christmas gift-giving when I was young. I don't blame them. Why give books when the children can simply download, with a library subscription or an account with an eBook-seller, the texts they want?

And yet, I reach my hand down into the ice-flanged sea of memory, and I pull out a copy of Elliot Paul's comic lost-generation-in-Paris mystery, *The Mysterious Mickey Finn*, that my older sister gave me the Christmas I was twelve, my introduction to the Dover catalogue of reprints of everything from Capablanca's chess memoirs to Leonardo da Vinci's drawings.

Like taking a core sample of a glacier, I can drill down the layers of past Christmas seasons to find Colin Wilson's *The Outsider*, an account of

cultural misfits that briefly seemed, when I was a teenager, the most meaningful thing I had ever read. And Robert Frost's *Collected Poems*, which took
years to appreciate. *Zorba the Greek*. Robert Heinlein's sci-fi juveniles. *Lord
Jim*. Back at the beginning, *A Child's Garden of Verses*. And toward the end
of childhood, Thomas à Kempis's *The Imitation of Christ*.

Christmas was books, and books Christmas, in those days now mostly
washed down to the cold sea. Was it such a bad way to grow up?

List of Illustrations